# This secret love-letter business . . .

**D**ear **D**iary,

Samantha received her first love note from her secret admirer.

Here is what the note said:

*Dear Samantha,* (I decided it was too soon to say "My dearest Samantha" — save that for later) *I have watched you from afar with a heavy heart. I am crazy about you. We live in the same neighborhood but go to different schools.* (I wanted her to think her secret admirer wasn't from Claremont.) *Writing this letter is the only way I can tell you how I feel. I wish you felt the same way about me.*

I signed it "Heartsore in Hampton Point," which I stole from a letter in the newspaper to Ann Landers.

Isn't that a terrific letter, Diary? But this secret love-letter business is complicated. . . .

# THE SECRET

# THE SECRET

## Carrie Randall

AN
**APPLE**
PAPERBACK

SCHOLASTIC INC.
New York Toronto London Auckland Sydney

ISBN 0-590-42477-7

Copyright © 1989 by Candice F. Ransom. All rights reserved. Published by Scholastic Inc. APPLE PAPERBACKS is a registered trademark of Scholastic Inc.

12 11 10 9 8 7 6 5 4 3 2 1          9/8 0 1 2 3 4/9

Printed in the U.S.A.                                    11

First Scholastic printing, November 1989

# THE SECRET

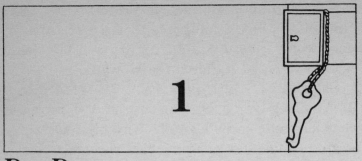

# 1

**D**ear **D**iary:

It's a good thing I have you, Diary. I got the most terrific idea in English today! But I can't tell anybody except you. Well, I told Nancy because she's my best friend, and we don't have any secrets. You wouldn't believe what Nancy did when I told her.

But I'm getting ahead of myself, as Gram says.

First, the idea. I'm going to *get even* with mean Samantha Howard. After what she did to me, she deserves it.

Here's how the idea came to me.

Mr. Rice asked us to write a paragraph about a special person. "Someone who has affected your life in a way you can't forget," he explained, writing a sample topic sentence on the board: *(Blank) is the most important person to me because (blank).*

It was the kind of assignment that sent pencils flying across notebook paper as kids wrote about fathers and mothers and big brothers and Aunt Hortenses. You wouldn't automatically think of your worst *enemy* as a special person, but that's when I thought of Samantha Howard.

She sits two rows over from me — the Queen of the Sixth Grade. She was twisting a strand of that long blonde hair as she scribbled her paragraph. I could just imagine what she was writing. *I am the most important person to me because I am so wonderful.* The dictionary could define "conceit" in two words: Samantha Howard.

I'm not mad at Samantha because she's stuck on herself or because she's a year older than the rest of us or even because she's boy-crazy and wears *makeup* (in the sixth grade).

I'm still mad at Samantha because she wrecked my very first slumber party. On *purpose.*

Anyway, back to class. I glanced down at the blank sheet of notebook paper on my desk. I would save myself a lot of trouble, not to mention a bad grade, by picking a safer subject than Samantha. My parents, for instance. Or my two older brothers, Adam, who's thirteen, and Joshua, who's sixteen. Or my two younger sisters, Rose, four, and Darcy, eight. Well, I probably wouldn't write about Darcy the pest. The most obvious choice is Gram. My family is loaded with special people.

Some really *were* special, like my grandmother, and some *thought* they were special, like my brother Josh.

Beside me, I could see that my best friend, Nancy, was also off to a slow start. We'd been friends since we were babies. Our mothers used to wheel us to the park in our strollers, so you could say we were friends before we could talk. I know Nancy like a book and she knows me pretty well, too.

Nancy's list of special people is much shorter than mine. She only has a mother and a father and no public enemies to speak of. Nancy's parents are divorced and Nancy lives a double life. Weekdays with her mom, and some weekends with her dad. She is forever choosing between them, like who to spend her birthday with. Maybe that was why she seemed stuck on her paragraph.

On her paper she had written in the top right-hand corner Nancy U. I used to sign my papers that way, with my first name and last initial (mainly because Miletti was hard to spell). Nancy hates her name and I don't blame her. Nancy Underpeace. Yuck. Boys are always calling her Underwear and Underpants.

Her topic sentence, I could see, was a real mess. But that's like Nancy. She has the worst handwriting in the world. She had crossed out three words and spelled *important* as *inportent*, even though it was right on the board.

Nancy erased furiously, her bottom lip caught between her teeth. Her eyebrows drew together in a frown.

"Mr. Rice marks down for holes," I whispered.

She looked up, frowning. "I don't care. What a dumb assignment. Why do we have to *write* a paragraph? Why can't we just *tell* about our special person?"

I didn't have any answer to that. Nancy always grumbles when we have to write in class. The teacher only gave us fifteen minutes. Knowing Nancy, she would erase and cross out and scribble until time was up and then ask Mr. Rice if she could finish hers at home.

"Who is yours about, Lizzie?" she asked, pressing on her pencil point so hard the lead snapped. Now she'd have to sharpen her pencil.

"I don't know. Gram, I guess." I looked at the clock. "I'd better hurry. Time's almost up."

"No, it isn't," Nancy said. "We've got eight minutes."

"We only have *four* minutes." Nancy always gets the time wrong. The clock was big as a kite — maybe she needs glasses. I sighed again. "We

4

started at twenty after. I wasted eleven minutes thinking about how I'd like to cut off Samantha's hair. Above her ears. With pinking shears."

"No, a dull knife," Nancy giggled.

One thing about Nancy, she has a great sense of humor. I couldn't have a friend who didn't. The slumber party a few weeks ago nearly ruined our friendship. Not that I could accuse Samantha of that. But it was Samantha who suggested I have the party in the first place. I eagerly agreed, I must admit, thinking Samantha wanted me to be in her crowd. It turned out Samantha had an ulterior motive. Nancy suspected things weren't on the up-and-up, as they say on TV. She came to my party anyway, even though she can't stand to be in the same zip code with Samantha.

Before the night was over Nancy and I had had a big fight, and Nancy stormed out. The rest of the evening quickly went downhill, especially after I figured out why Samantha *really* wanted to come to my house . . . just to flirt with my brother Adam.

I made up with Nancy, and now everything is like it used to be. But the memory of our fight and that awful party still bothers me.

Anyway, back to this afternoon. Suddenly the terrific idea hit me.

"I want revenge," I said. "I have to make Samantha pay for what she did to me. Who was it that said revenge is sweet?"

"Rambo." Nancy gave up on her paper entirely, crumpling it into a wad.

The more I thought about getting even, the more I liked the idea, even though I know it isn't nice. It fit in with my November Resolution (I can't wait until January). I have decided to take control of my own life.

I read all about control in this magazine of Mom's. There was an article called "Take Control of Your Own Life." It was for women who have jobs and children and ovens to clean and feel like they're going crazy. Just the way I do sometimes! Even though I'm too young to have a job, and I don't have to clean the oven.

You know what life is like in our family, Diary. Little sisters and yelling brothers and too many pets. It's like living in a hurricane.

Anyway, this article said the way to get control of your life is to *make* things happen instead of letting things happen *to* you. So I'm going to make Samantha Howard pay for ruining my party. And then I'll be in control of my own life.

When school first started this year I wanted to be cool, like Samantha and her friends, Candace Quinn and Jessica Aldridge. The three of them sort of run sixth grade. Samantha has it all together. That girl knows exactly what she's doing every minute of every day. She made me have the slumber party so she could hang around my brother Adam. She just *used* me.

"Pass your papers forward, please," Mr. Rice announced, interrupting my thoughts. "You've had ample time. In fact, I gave you an extra two minutes."

Nancy's hand was in the air. "Can I bring mine in tomorrow? My pencil broke."

"I would have been happy to lend you a pencil, Nancy," he said, collecting the papers from the first row.

"I know, but I got stuck anyway. It's hard to write about a special person in only fifteen minutes." Nancy always has a steady supply of excuses. She never seems to run out.

"Mr. Rice," I said, using the opportunity Nancy opened for me. "I didn't finish my paper, either. I'll work on it during lunch — "

"Bring it in immediately after lunch," he said, irritated. "Everyone else was able to complete their assignments. I don't know why you two couldn't."

Samantha turned around and smirked.

I would have stuck my tongue out at her, but that was babyish, and anyway I was afraid Mr.

Rice would figure Nancy and I didn't finish our papers because we were busy talking, and move one of us. I couldn't afford to be separated from Nancy, not now. If I was going to get even with Samantha Howard, I needed all the help I could get.

Of course, I didn't know then that Nancy had no intention of helping me.

During lunch I worked on my paragraph, wondering why mine was due on Mr. Rice's desk right after the bell, yet Nancy had until the next day.

I finished my peanut butter sandwich. "How do you do it?" I asked.

"Do what?"

"Get Mr. Rice to let you turn your assignments in late."

Nancy shrugged. "No big deal. You said you had to talk to me about something. What is it?"

"Just a sec." I quickly wrote about the special person in my life, my grandmother. I chose her because she *was* special and I wouldn't use up a lot of time thinking about what to write.

Gram lives upstairs in her own apartment in our house. She's a widow. Grandpa died twelve years ago, before I was born. Gram is more than a grandmother — she's my good friend. I think she remembers what it was like to be my age, which makes her easy to talk to.

I jotted my name at the top, hoping Mr. Rice would think six sentences was enough. I had more important business to discuss with Nancy.

"I've decided to get back at Samantha," I said, keeping my voice down since the Queen of the Sixth Grade was sitting at the table behind us.

"Oh, yeah. You were going to chop her hair off."

"No, I mean *really* get back at her."

Nancy swallowed her milk in surprise. "You're serious."

"You bet I am." I sounded brave, but inside I was nervous.

"Are you sure you want to do this, Lizzie? Samantha probably has friends in high places. She might make *you* pay."

"I already have!" I lowered my voice again. "I can't let her get away with making me look like a turkey. The only reason Samantha asked me to have the party was so she could hang around my brother. I should have guessed she had a crush on Adam, but I didn't until it was too late."

"It could happen to anyone," Nancy said. She's *always* loyal . . . well, almost always. "Samantha is full of tricks. Maybe when we're twelve, we'll be that cool and smart," Nancy added.

I didn't want to wait a whole year to be cool and smart and in control. "Samantha has to learn she can't push me around."

Nancy stared at me. "Lizzie, what is with you all of a sudden? You're not the mean-and-nasty type. In fact, you're the nicest, most soft-hearted person I know."

One thing about Nancy, she always smacks the truth squarely on the head.

I *am* nice and soft-hearted. Too nice, maybe. Like, if a room-mother brings in twenty-nine cupcakes and there are thirty kids in the class, the teacher will always ask *me* if I don't mind not having one. Because he knows I won't complain. Good old Lizzie Milleti. She won't care. She doesn't mind being last, or taking the worst seat, or getting the smallest helping.

That's the way it's always been. Not just at school, but at home, too.

It was time to draw the line and take charge of my life.

"Why should I be nice to Samantha?" I told Nancy. "She wasn't very nice to me, wrecking my party."

"Okay, so you're going to get back at her. Have you thought of a plan, Mastermind?"

"As a matter of fact, I have." I leaned forward

so you-know-who wouldn't overhear. "Samantha likes Adam, right? Suppose she got notes from him. Love letters, sort of."

Nancy's eyes widened. "Adam is going to write love letters to Samantha? Not the Adam Miletti I know. Besides, eighth-graders don't fall in love with sixth-graders. Even if the sixth-grader looks like Samantha."

"Of course Adam won't write love letters to Samantha," I said scornfully. "Adam won't know anything about the letters. *I'll* write them. But I need your help. I want you to copy the notes so they'll be in a different handwriting."

Nancy looked like our St. Bernard did whenever somebody mentioned the word "vet" — kind of panicky. "What's wrong with your handwriting?" she asked warily.

"Well, look at it." I pushed my special person paper toward her. "It's too girly. Samantha would know in a minute that Adam didn't write the notes. But your handwriting is — " I stopped. I didn't want to hurt Nancy's feelings by saying that her handwriting looked more like my brother's, chicken-scratchy. " — better than mine," I finished lamely.

"Forget it." Nancy crunched up her lunch bag.

"What do you mean, 'forget it'?"

"Just what I said. I don't want any part of your scheme." She got up and walked over to the trash bins without another word.

"Nancy — !" I was shocked. Nancy was always saying how she'd like to see snooty old Samantha taken down a peg or two. Here was the perfect chance to make Samantha look bad and Nancy didn't want any part of it!

Maybe Nancy felt she was in control of her life. I mean, she's the tallest kid in class so she's never been called "shrimp" the way I have. Plus her hair is thick and blonde and straight, the complete opposite of mine. At least her hair *was* straight, before she got a perm a few weeks ago. You can tell from a person's hair how much control they have over their life. Mine is a brown frizzball, so it's no surprise that my life is a mess. And Nancy seems to have Mr. Rice in the palm of her hand, being allowed to turn in her assignments late. Nancy didn't need to get back at Samantha — Samantha hadn't done anything to *her*.

A loud laugh made me turn around. Samantha was laughing at something Donald Harrington said. Donald was the drippiest boy in sixth grade, but Samantha gazed at him like he was Billy Watts, the cutest boy in the whole school. Obviously she wasn't pining away for my brother. I had to act fast, with or without Nancy, before Samantha became interested in somebody else.

The minute I got home, I tossed my books onto the kitchen table and ran up to the second floor.

"Gram, you home?" I shouted at the bottom of the attic stairs. Gram sold real estate. Sometimes she was out showing houses.

"Yes, come on up," came Gram's voice.

I clattered up the steps, grateful to get away from the racket that Baby Rose and Darcy were making in the living room. Rose is only four, so she had an excuse, but Darcy is old enough to play fairly with the baby instead of causing her to scream. I knew when Mom came up from the basement (she does at least two loads of laundry every single day in our house), she'd ask me to fold clothes or entertain Rose, and I wasn't wild about doing either.

My grandmother's attic apartment is an oasis of quiet in our noisy house. The little kids visit Gram, but nobody comes up here as often as I do. Gram is wonderful to all of us kids, but I secretly believe she likes me the best. I was named Elizabeth after her. People call Gram Betty but they call me Lizzie. I'm thinking about having my name legally changed to Lizbeth.

At the top of the stairs, I paused to pet Trouble, one of Gram's cats. She has two cats, Trouble and Mischief, who had her kittens in the dryer last month. The kittens will soon be ready to be given away to good homes. Nancy has dibs on the black-and-white one. We also have two cats, Marilyn Monroe and Elvis, plus good old Sebastian. As the only dog, he puts up with a lot from all those cats.

"Hi, Gram," I said, entering my grandmother's apartment. "I wrote about you in English today. And I got an 85 on that fractions test I was so worried about. We're starting track next week in gym. Ugh!"

Gram was standing in front of the long oval mirror by the bureau. She was holding her best dress in front of her, studying her reflection as if she had never seen herself before.

"Hello, Lizzie," she murmured, without taking her eyes off the mirror.

I collapsed on the bed. "Ms. Donnally put up this chart in gym. Every week she's going to write down the miles we run. Miles, Gram! Some of the guys are trying for fifty miles! Of course, they've got the whole year to do it. The least you can run is ten miles. I probably won't make that by June." I groaned. "Do you think track and field qualifies as cruel and inhuman punishment?"

Now Gram held up a shiny black shoe to check

14

the effect against the beige of her dress. "Yes," she said, smiling to herself. "It looks just right."

"Gram!" I cried in anguish. "Haven't you heard a word I said?"

"What?" She turned from the mirror. "I'm sorry, dear. What did you say?"

Then I noticed the blue-and-gold shoe-store bags on the floor. "You went shopping!" I cried. "You promised we'd go Saturday."

"Did I?" She pulled a black purse from a nest of tissue paper. The purse matched the shoes. Opening the purse, she absently examined the satin interior. "I really don't remember. . . ."

"How could you forget? First we were going to the card shop and then we were going to the bookstore and then we were going to have lunch at — "

She closed her new purse with a snap. "Oh, Lizzie, I can't go shopping with you Saturday. I'm sorry, dear, but I've made other plans. I truly forgot we were supposed to go shopping. You don't mind, do you? We'll go another time."

I *did* mind, terribly, but instead of throwing a fit like Rose did whenever she didn't get her way, I asked, "Where are you going, Gram?"

"Where am I going?" she echoed.

"Yeah. Do you have to show a house Saturday or what?" I was a little annoyed with her. What

15

was with my on-the-ball grandmother? She was acting weird.

"No, I don't have to show a house," she replied vaguely. "I'm just going — out."

It was obvious she wasn't about to tell me any more. I watched her carefully place her new shoes back in the tissue-lined box. "I thought you didn't like black, Gram."

"Well, I changed my mind," she replied, stowing the shoe box and purse bag in her closet. "Lizzie, I have to make a call. Would you mind going back downstairs?"

What was so private I couldn't hear? But I went downstairs, feeling hurt. Gram always puts me first. She never asks me to take the worst seat or accept the smallest helping. She is the one person who understands that sometimes I *need* to be first.

At least, she *used* to be.

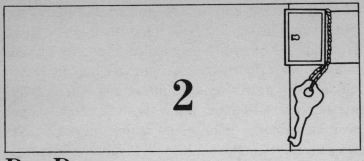

**2**

**D**ear **D**iary:

English class was *soooo* boring today, so I worked on the first love letter. I know, I'm supposed to do English stuff in English class, but in a way, I *was*. Mr. Rice is always telling us to write more.

I decided that Samantha would receive a series of notes from a secret admirer. Knowing Samantha, she'll show the letters to everybody in the state. She's not the type to keep quiet about a secret admirer. Then, when the time is right, I'll write the last letter, the one that will reveal the truth. That there *is* no secret admirer. Samantha will look like the biggest nerd!

The hard part was making my letter sound like it was from my brother without actually *saying* it was from Adam. The notes had to be anonymous, but Samantha had to *think* they were from Adam or my whole plan wouldn't work.

So far I had jotted on a piece of scratch paper,

*My dearest Samantha, I have watched you from afar with a heavy heart* — That line was straight from an old movie. I especially liked the phrase "heavy heart." Picturing Adam writing such stuff made me giggle. I could almost see Adam dragging around this great big Valentine heart. Adam would probably dribble the Valentine heart the way he dribbles the basketball he always has with him.

"What's so funny?" Nancy whispered. We were speaking to each other again — the incident at lunch yesterday was sort of mutually forgotten.

I muffled my giggles. "It's this note I'm working on. The one to Samantha? I just thought of something funny. Are you sure you don't want to help? It's going to be such a riot, watching her think Adam is crazy in love with her."

Nancy shook her head. "I told you yesterday I don't like the idea of getting back at people."

"I don't know when you got so high and mighty," I retorted. "If Samantha Howard ruined *your* slumber party, I'd be the first person to help you get revenge."

She glanced over at the note I had started, then looked away without saying anything.

Just then Mr. Rice cleared his throat to make a special announcement.

"Class," he said, "as you know, Claremont Elementary sends a contribution to Children's Hospital every year around holiday time. Miss Tyler's class is having a bake sale — "

"That the kids' mothers have to bake for," Nancy muttered. "My mom says she's glad I'm not in her class this year."

"The fourth-graders are raking lawns," Mr. Rice went on. "Mr. Devon's class is holding a car wash." That was the other sixth-grade class. "I thought we'd do something different. For our project, we are going to have a one-day Read-A-Thon."

"Read-a-*what*?" asked Howie Strauch.

"Read-A-Thon," Mr. Rice repeated.

"Sounds like *work*," grumbled Donald Harrington.

"I guarantee it'll be easier than washing cars." Mr. Rice sat on the edge of his desk, jiggling a piece of chalk in his hand. "How many of you have seen a telethon?" Nearly everyone's hand shot into the air. "Okay. The principle of our Read-A-Thon is the same. Only we won't be on television. People will pledge a sum of money to our project, which will be reading books. Each of you will decide how many pages you can read in a single day. Then you will ask people to pledge money, based on your goal."

About half the class gave a puzzled "Huh?"

Mr. Rice turned to the board. "Let's say you decide to read fifty pages. You'll take around a pledge sheet, which I will make up and run off." He sketched a rough chart. "For every ten pages you promise to read, people will pledge a dollar. But if you reach your goal of fifty pages, the person will pay, say, ten dollars, *if* they want to pledge the whole amount. Let people know in the beginning that they don't have to pledge that much. However, I think a lot of people will be impressed with your ambition and will probably pledge the entire amount. Any questions?"

There were a million questions. What if we didn't want to read fifty pages? What kinds of books did we have to read? Could we read comic books? Did *Mad* magazine count? What if we didn't reach our goal? What if we couldn't get anybody to sign up? Couldn't we sell cookies instead?

Mr. Rice promised he would make up dittos explaining the rules, and pledge sheets so we could start signing people up right away. He set the date of our one-day Read-A-Thon, December 20, our next-to-last day of school before Christmas vacation.

"We won't have to do any work that whole day," I said to Nancy. "Except read whatever we want. Won't that be fun?"

She threw her pencil down. "I think it's stupid. Why can't we do something normal to raise money? Like a dog wash. People won't pay money for us to read books. They won't even *see* us, so how will they know they're getting their money's worth?"

"Mr. Rice will watch us," I said. "He won't let us cheat. Anyway, who'd want to cheat? Reading is easy."

"It's just a sneaky way of getting us to work." Nancy slammed her notebook in disgust.

I figured she didn't like the idea of collecting people's pledges. Some kids hated going door-to-door, even for a good cause. I planned to make a quick little speech using some of my father's sales tactics. Dad is a salesman for Roth Frozen Foods. He has a lot of techniques to convince people that Asparagus Pizza Squares would be a hot seller in their stores.

To me, collecting pledges would be more fun than the actual Read-A-Thon. But even if Nancy didn't agree, we'd go around together. We do everything together . . . except get back at Samantha Howard. Maybe if I offered to help Nancy collect pledges, she'd change her mind and help me with the notes.

"Listen," I said to her. "When we get the sign-up sheets let's start right away in our neighborhood. We won't have to split up and take different streets. Our neighbors are so nice, they'll probably pledge for both of us. We might get more pledges than anybody." I was laying it on pretty thick, but Nancy still seemed hesitant.

"Okay?" I persisted when she didn't answer.

"I'm busy tomorrow afternoon," Nancy replied at last.

I didn't know about any plans. "Doing what?"

Her lips were set in a tense line. "Do I give you the third degree about every little thing you do, Lizzie Miletti?"

I drew back as if she'd slapped me. "Well, no, but I thought it'd be fun if we went together — "

"Not tomorrow."

"What about the next day?"

"I'm busy then, too." She rummaged busily in her knapsack, not looking at me.

I was silent, stung with hurt. Clearly Nancy did not want to go around the neighborhood with me to sign up pledges. She didn't want to help me get revenge on Samantha Howard, either. I can't help thinking that maybe she doesn't want to be my friend anymore. And I can't imagine life without Nancy.

\* \* \*

Most of my family was out in the yard when I got home from school. If you were just driving by, there'd be no doubt in your mind that the Milettis lived in the house on the corner.

One time we were all in the front yard, just noodling around, and this man pulled his car over to the curb and yelled, "Why has a crowd gathered? What's going on?" I was so embarrassed — the crowd was my *family*.

Josh was waxing Mom's car. Now that he's sixteen and has his driver's license, he keeps Mom's car showroom-spiffy. Adam was shooting baskets. Nothing unusual about that. J.V. try-outs were coming up and he wanted to make the team.

Mom and Darcy were raking leaves. Even little Rose was "helping," picking up leaves from the big pile and carefully placing them back under the trees. The cats were taking turns jumping in the leaf pile, while Sebastian lay in the driveway, sniffing the air with his big nose.

"Where's Gram?" I asked Mom. "I thought she'd be outside on a great day like this."

"Out," Mom replied in a tone that warned me not to ask where.

Rose ran over to present me with a leaf bouquet. "For you, Lizzie."

"Thank you." I pretended to smell the "flowers."

"Mom, she's doing it again," Darcy yelled. "Make Rose quit messing up my leaf pile!"

My mother sighed. "Now I know why they call this time of year 'fall.' Everything falls on the ground for me to rake."

"Look, look!" Rose shrieked.

We all tipped our heads back to see a huge flock of birds fly over the rooftops. I wished Nancy could see this — she loved birds. But she was off on the mysterious errand she wouldn't tell me about.

"Where are they going?" Darcy wanted to know.

"South," I answered.

"Why are they going south?" was her next question. Darcy asked more questions than a poll-taker.

"Because," I said, knowing that would never be good enough for my inquisitive sister.

She tugged Mom's sleeve. "Why are the birds going south?"

"Because it's time for them to go," Mom answered. She has loads more patience with Darcy than I'll ever have. "They spend their winters in warmer climates so they have food. It snows here and covers up their food supply."

"Lizzie," Josh called. "Hand me that rag."

I picked up a cloth lying on the sidewalk and

24

gave it to him. He began shining the chrome vigorously. I figured he was washing and waxing Mom's car for a good reason, so he could go cruising — his main occupation since he got his driver's license.

I envy my oldest brother. Josh is the first of us kids to escape the family. He's free as a bird — when Mom lets him borrow her car. At least he has *some* control over his life.

Shielding my eyes from the bright sun slanting across the roof, I watched Adam sink basket after basket. "Do you think Adam will ever get interested in girls?" I casually asked Josh.

"Sure. Give him time. He's only thirteen. He's got a lot of growing up to do." Josh said this as if he were finished with growing up himself. Sometimes he can be *so* superior.

A horrible thought dawned on me. Suppose Adam really *liked* Samantha Howard! It wasn't totally impossible, even for Adam. Samantha might be two years behind Adam in school, but she was only a year behind him in age and *very* sophisticated. Not to mention beautiful. Instead of making Samantha look like a jerk, my notes could bring them together.

I walked over to the garage. "Hi," I said.

"Hi." Adam didn't spare me a glance. I'm used to being ignored. If Adam has his basketball in his hand, which he does about twenty-three hours a day, nothing else exists.

"What do you think of Samantha Howard?" I asked point-blank. No sense beating around the bush.

"Who?"

"Sa*man*tha. The girl who lives on the next street? With the long blonde hair?"

"Oh, *that* one." Obviously Samantha had made some kind of an impression on my brother.

"Yes, *that* one. What do you think of her?"

He shrugged before lining up another shot. "She's just a girl."

Samantha would die if she heard Adam say she was just a girl! But I felt reassured.

"Lizzie," Mom said. "Come rake the rest of this section for me. I have to go in and start supper."

I hate to rake leaves. "What about Adam? He's not doing anything."

"The boys promised to rake the backyard, which is the worst."

I wished Gram were there. She makes even the worst jobs seem like fun. "When's Gram coming back?"

Mom climbed the steps. "I don't know. She didn't tell me."

"She must have told you *some*thing."

"Honestly, Lizzie, you ask more questions than

Darcy!" Mom said, annoyed. "Your grandmother is a grown person. She doesn't have to check in with me." Mom went inside, shutting the door behind her with more force than necessary.

I leaned on the rake, puzzled. Why was everyone acting so strange? First Nancy, then Gram, and now my mother.

I wish I knew what was going on, Diary. I don't like things to change. Dad says I ought to be a Republican when I grow up, because Republicans don't like anything that hasn't happened before. I'm not sure what that means, but I *do* know I feel uneasy.

Gram didn't come home for supper. She didn't always eat with us, since she had her own little kitchen upstairs, but she usually shared at least part of her day with the family.

After dinner, I loaded the dishwasher. For once our house was relatively quiet. Darcy was taking a bath. Mom was reading a bedtime story to Rose. Adam was in his room listening to his stereo. And Josh was at the library. Even the cats were out. The only person keeping me company was Sebastian, and he doesn't technically qualify as a person. He snoozed in front of the refrigerator.

While I rinsed the plates, I punched Nancy's phone number. Her mother answered.

"Is Nancy there?" I asked Mrs. Underpeace.

"She's out right now," Nancy's mother told me. "She won't be back until eight or so."

"Oh. Please tell her I called, Mrs. Underpeace." I hung up. Did Nancy have *another* mysterious appointment? She could be at her father's, but her mother would have said so. It wasn't a deep dark secret if Nancy visited her father.

Nancy is having trouble adjusting to the divorce. Not so much the fact that her parents broke up — she seems to understand that pretty well. Her biggest problem is her father. He practically wears her out on weekend visits, taking her to the zoo, the movies, museums, shopping, out to eat every single meal. I went with her to her dad's once, so I knew she wasn't exaggerating when she complained she needed to check into a rest home after weekends with her father.

Maybe Nancy's mother had to work late today. She didn't like to leave Nancy alone, so maybe she'd arranged for Nancy to spend the evening with her father. But Nancy could have stayed with us. Mom cooks enough for an army, and she's forever telling Mrs. Underpeace how Nancy is always welcome in our house. Where *was* Nancy?

As I poured dishwashing powder into the cup, my father walked into the kitchen. He set a box on the table. Inwardly I cringed. It was probably another experimental Roth Frozen Food. Dad tests all the new products on us. We are his guinea pigs.

I tried to slip past him, but Sebastian chose that moment to trip me. "Dumb dog!" I cried.

Dad helped me up. "See this box, Lizzie?"

I couldn't bear to look at it. Whatever it contained, I would probably have to eat it sooner or later.

"We've been scooped," Dad said, tapping the box. "Christmas Crispies."

I forced myself to look then. "That's cereal. Your company doesn't make cereal." Or anything else a sensible person would eat.

"I know, but this other company scooped my idea to put out a special snack product just for Christmas. I've been trying to convince management for a year that people would go for something like this. And now someone else has done it."

"It probably won't sell." To take his mind off Christmas Crispies, I asked him a question that had been on my mind. "Dad, what's the best way to control your life?"

"Get into management."

"Dad! I'm serious."

He opened the Christmas Crispies and sampled a handful. "Not bad. Lizzie, everybody likes to believe they can control their own lives, so there isn't any single, accepted way to do it. But there is a key."

"What is it?" I asked eagerly.

"Knowledge."

Now it was my turn to sigh. "I suppose you're going to start on how important it is to have an education. Boy, you and Mom sneak that into the conversation every chance you get — "

"Knowledge gives you control," Dad insisted. "If you know things, you are able to make better decisions."

I didn't really want to hear a lecture on the value of education. Hastily mopping the counters clean, I left my father alone in the kitchen, morosely eating handful after handful of Christmas Crispies.

Gram came in after I was in bed. I hopped out and ran to her door, anxious to find out where she'd been all this time.

"It's late," she told me on her way to her room. "I'll talk to you in the morning."

But she didn't. She slept in the next morning, and I went to school. Nancy wouldn't tell me where *she'd* been, either. When I got home from school, Gram was gone again! *Everyone* seems to have a secret!

Mom was tightlipped on the subject, but I could

tell she was upset. After all, it was *her* mother staying out all hours of the night. I wouldn't like it if Mom kept coming home late.

Even Darcy noticed things were different. Tonight she sat on the edge of the tub while I got ready for bed.

"What's wrong with Mom?" she asked me. "She doesn't answer my questions."

"Sure she does," I said, not wanting her to worry. "Just today I heard her tell you why the sun rises in the east."

Darcy twisted her Snoopy pajamas in a knot. "She answers *some* of my questions but not *all* of my questions. Not the important ones."

I know just how she felt. The important questions are being swept under the rug. There is only one way to learn the answers.

I am going to find out myself where my grandmother is disappearing to every night.

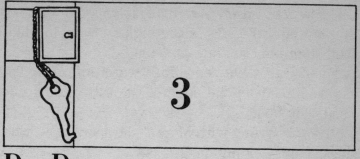

**3**

**D**ear **D**iary:

Today started out to be a great day, but it didn't end up that way.

I'll tell you about the good part first.

Samantha received her first love note from her secret admirer. Just seeing her face as she read it made staying up half the night to copy the note over worthwhile.

Here is what the note said:

*Dear Samantha,* (I decided it was too soon to say "My dearest Samantha" — save that for later) *I have watched you from afar with a heavy heart. I am crazy about you. We live in the same neighborhood, but go to different schools.* (I wanted her to think her secret admirer wasn't from Claremont.) *Writing this letter is the only way I can tell you how I feel. I wish you felt the same way about me. If I have the nerve, I might write to you again.*

I signed it "Heartsore in Hampton Point," which I stole from a letter in the newspaper to Ann Landers.

Isn't that a terrific letter, Diary? Samantha will go nuts trying to figure out who is crazy about her. And the letter is just a little sad, which will make her sympathetic.

But this secret love-letter business is complicated. After I wrote a rough draft, I had to copy it over. If only Nancy was around. Her handwriting is sloppy like Adam's. But she wasn't around and anyway, she'd made it clear she didn't want any part of my plan to get back at Samantha. So I went into the room Adam shared with Josh, holding my nose because of the smelly socks lying all over the floor, and found an English assignment Adam had thrown in the trash. Using his paper as an example, I copied my note over in a pretty good imitation of his chicken-scratch handwriting.

Then I had to deliver the letter. That was tough. If we had lockers like they do in junior high, I could just slip the note through the vent in Samantha's locker. But we don't have lockers. In class we have an open cupboard with hooks for our coats and knapsacks. I thought about sticking the envelope in Samantha's coat pocket, but then she would have suspected it came from somebody in Claremont, probably her class.

Finally I decided to do what the teachers do when they need to send a message: use a first-grader. The little kids are forever running between classrooms and the office with envelopes clenched in their hands. They also deliver notes from the junior high, which is right next door to our school.

In the mornings the buses stop at both schools, letting kids off at Claremont before going on to the junior high. Lots of times the junior high kids pass messages to kids in Claremont, using a first-grader as a messenger.

I found a likely looking candidate trying to get a drink from the big kids' fountain.

"Do you know Samantha Howard?" I asked in a stern voice. "She's a sixth-grader, tall, with long blonde hair."

The little girl nodded solemnly.

"Give this to her when she comes in, will you?" Samantha usually walks to school with Candace Quinn and Jessica Aldridge. She always makes a grand entrance, so it's impossible to miss her.

"It's very important," I told the little girl, handing her the envelope. "Don't say anything, even if she asks you where it came from. Pretend you don't know. Just give her the note. Okay?"

Again the girl nodded. I've learned from experience that if you sound official, like a teacher, little kids will do what you want. First-graders are in awe of the big kids.

Nancy came into the building, her cheeks pink from her brisk bike ride. I think riding bikes to school is babyish, but Nancy still does it. Nancy thinks sixth grade is just like fifth grade, only with harder homework. I know sixth grade is more than that. It's our last year to fool around, but it's also sort of a practice year for junior high.

Nancy doesn't see it that way. She still rides her bike and climbs trees and goofs off. She admits she likes being a kid. "I'm good at it," she says. "I probably won't be any good as a teenager." I might not be that great myself, but I want to try it at least.

Nancy spotted me standing near the bulletin board next to the office and came over.

"Hey, Lizzie!" Her voice boomed around the hall. "How's it going?"

"Shhhh!" I hissed at her.

She pulled off her stocking cap. Her hair, half-grown out from the perm, was all fly-away from electricity. "What's with you?"

"I'm waiting for Samantha to get her note," I whispered hoarsely. "I'd rather not call attention to myself." I turned toward the bulletin board, pretending to be fascinated by the second-grade display of pilgrims and turkeys.

Nancy adopted the same pose. "How is she getting the note?" she asked, speaking out of the side of her mouth like a gangster in an old movie.

"The little kid in the red sweater. She's supposed to hand it to her. I didn't want Samantha to think the note came from somebody in this school."

Nancy punched me in the arm. She does that a lot. Sometimes I wish Nancy would hurry up and grow up. "Dumbhead! In case you haven't noticed, that little kid is from this school!"

"Yes, but the *buses* go to both schools. A junior high boy could have passed the note to a kid from this school," I explained. "Samantha knows that. I told her not to say anything, just give Samantha the note."

The doors opened, letting in a blast of chilly early-morning air and Samantha Howard. She breezed in like she had just won the Miss America pageant. Jessica and Candace flanked her on either side, like bodyguards.

I grabbed Nancy excitedly. "Don't look! We can't let her see us!" We stood so close to the bulletin board the tail of a construction paper turkey tickled my nose.

"Here," the little kid said to Samantha. My heart leaped into my throat, but the girl didn't say another word.

"What's this?" Samantha demanded. "Who's it from? Who gave you this?"

The little girl walked down the hall without answering.

"Hey, kid!" Samantha called.

"A letter!" Candace cried. "Samantha's in trouble!"

"Uh-oh," Jessica piped up. "I bet it's a note from Ms. Donnally. Sam's flunking gym."

"Quit pushing," Samantha ordered. "I can't open it."

I couldn't resist. I had to see what was going on. I turned around very slowly. In the middle of the lobby, Samantha ripped open the envelope I had sealed so carefully. Her expression changed as she quickly read the message inside.

"It's not from Ms. Donnally," she said mysteriously, looking at her friends with a smile like a cat (if a cat could smile).

"Who's it from?" Candace tried to see the letter.

Samantha held it out of reach. "That's for me to know and you to find out," she teased.

"Samantha!" Jessica and Candace chorused, outraged.

Samantha minced down the hall. "Just somebody who's madly in love with me, that's who," she said smugly.

Candace and Jessica ran after her, dying of curiosity. Nobody saw us by the bulletin board.

My little messenger came over. "Did I do okay?" she asked.

"You did great." I gave her a new pack of gum I happened to have in my pocket. "Thanks a lot."

I clutched Nancy's shoulders, laughing so hard I could barely stand. "She fell for it! Samantha actually fell for it! I can't believe it!"

"I can't either," Nancy said, wonderingly. "I have to admit, it's a pretty good scheme, Lizzie."

"Then why don't you help me?" I said. "I have lots of notes to write yet."

Before Nancy could reply, Mr. Rice came out of the office. He carried a stack of dittos.

"Hello, girls," he greeted us.

"Hello, Mr. Rice," I said. "Are those the sign-up sheets for the Read-A-Thon?"

He nodded. "Sign-up sheets and instructions. I need a couple of helpers to staple and collate. Would you girls like to volunteer?"

Doing Mr. Rice's office chores was fun. I turned to Nancy, but suddenly she bolted out the front door, mumbling something about checking her bike lock.

Mr. Rice looked at me. "Well. I guess it's just you, Lizzie."

I stared at the swinging front door. "Yes," I

said to the empty air where Nancy had been. "I guess it's just me."

Diary, it seems the whole world is keeping secrets from me. Nancy, my grandmother, even my mother. After Nancy's strange behavior today, I came home from school determined to find out *some*thing.

I was thrilled to see Gram's car in the driveway, pulled up in front of Mom's. That meant Gram wasn't planning to go out anymore today.

I said a quick hello to my mother, who was in the kitchen fixing dinner, then ran up to Gram's apartment. I was anxious to tell her how weird Nancy had been acting lately. Maybe Gram would know what was wrong with Nancy. Sometimes Nancy confided in Gram. My grandmother is the world's best listener and problem-solver. She ought to charge a fee but I'm glad she doesn't, because I'd be broke!

From behind the closed bathroom door in Gram's apartment, I heard water running into the tub. Gram was singing a tuneless little song. She sounded happy. Then I noticed her good beige dress hanging in the doorway. Sitting beneath the dress were her new black shoes and purse. Maybe she *was* going out again.

Through the bathroom door I said, "Gram? It's me, Lizzie. Are you on your way someplace?"

"I sure am," Gram sang over the running tap. The door opened and she poked her head out. She wore her black lace shower cap, which meant she had been to the beauty parlor. "Would you bring me a facecloth, dear? I forgot one."

I brought her a facecloth. When I handed it to her, she said thanks and closed the door firmly. If she had hung a do-not-disturb sign on the door, I couldn't have gotten the message more clearly. She wasn't going to tell me where she was going.

It wasn't that my grandmother never went anywhere. She showed property all the time. She often got together with women from work to go to the movies. And she went to the Y to swim. Going out wasn't strange. What was strange was the way she was trying to hide it.

Downstairs Mom rattled pots and pans extra loud, obviously in a bad mood or mad about something. Maybe Gram hadn't told *her* where she was going either, and Mom was peeved over it. After all, Gram was Mom's very own mother. Family ties ought to count for something.

There was only one way to see for myself what Gram was up to — spy on her. Okay, spying is low-down and sneaky. I know that. But how else could I find out what was going on?

40

I went down to my room. When I heard Gram's high heels click down the steps, I ran to the windows that looked out on the street.

A car I had never seen before rolled up in front of our house. A big blue car with a noisy engine. As I watched, a man got out of the driver's side and walked briskly up our sidewalk. Looking down, I could see the top of his head, which was bald, and his shiny shoes poking out from under a little pot-bellied stomach. He reminded me of a cookie jar, kind of dumpling-shaped.

The front door opened and closed. Seconds later, Gram and the man came out on the sidewalk. They smiled at each other, and then he took Gram's arm and tucked it into the bend of his own arm. They walked like this all the way to the car. The man helped Gram into the passenger seat, then he walked around to the driver's side and got in. They drove off in a cloud of exhaust.

I couldn't stand it another second. Marching into the kitchen, I blurted to my mother, "*Who* is that man Gram just left with?"

She glanced at me over the pot she was stirring. "Oh, you saw Mr. Bagnold?"

"Mr. Bagnold? Is that his name? Who is he?"

"He works with Gram. He's new at her agency."

"Oh, then Gram is helping him out." When a new kid starts school late, the teacher assigns someone to take the new kid around for a few days, show him the ropes.

Mom looked at me oddly. "I wouldn't exactly call it helping."

"What *would* you call it?"

"Dating," she said flatly.

I nearly choked. "What?" I gasped.

"Your grandmother is going to a Spencer Tracy film festival with Mr. Bagnold," Mom explained. "I believe they call that a date."

"Gram, out on a date?" My voice scaled upward until I sounded as shrill as Rose. "But she's so — " I meant to say "old," but Gram didn't *act* like an old lady. She wasn't like those grandmothers who sit in a rocking chair, knitting. But still . . . *dating?*

My mother guessed what I was thinking. "There is no age limit to dating. Gram is an attractive woman. She's bright and fun to be with. You shouldn't be surprised that she is seeing a man."

"Aren't you?" She was, I could tell.

Mom sighed. "It's been so long since my dad died — I thought she'd never be interested in anyone else." She gazed into the distance. "I suppose she needs companionship."

"She doesn't need companionship," I said. "She's got us."

"Maybe we're not enough anymore," my mother said, somewhat sadly.

I can't believe my grandmother is out on a date, this very minute!

It's just too embarrassing to think about, Diary. No matter what Mom said, grandmothers don't date!

# 4

**D**ear **D**iary:

I just couldn't stand it yesterday after Mom told me that Gram was *dating* That Man. I stayed up until she got home, which wasn't very late, and then I went upstairs. I had to know if what my mother said was true. This is what happened.

Gram was in a bubbly mood. "Lizzie!" she cried as if she hadn't seen me in years. "Sit down and talk to me, while I change out of this dress."

"Did you have a good time?" I hinted.

"Wonderful! Simply wonderful!" she said.

I sat down on her bed while Gram wiggled out of her dress and pantyhose, and waited for her to say more. She put on her old bathrobe and fuzzy slippers. Usually that was the signal for us to go downstairs and have cookies and milk. Instead Gram wandered around the room, humming to herself. She was smiling, too, a special smile I had never seen before.

If anyone was going to break into the subject,

it would have to be me. "Where did you go?" I asked, stroking Trouble, who had jumped into my lap. Both cats and several kittens swarmed around my ankles, craving attention. I didn't blame them. The cats weren't the only ones neglected around here lately.

Gram picked up one of Mischief's kittens — the one Nancy was taking — and kissed its tiny pink nose. "We went to a little Greek restaurant first, and then to a film festival featuring Spencer Tracy." She sighed. "He used to be my favorite actor. I just loved him in *Captains Courageous*. He won an Academy Award that year. Hello, Oscar, you cute thing." Holding the kitten high, she added, "I think Ralph looks a little like him."

"Who?" All those names confused me.

"Ralph Bagnold. The man who took me to the movies this evening."

"Ralph Bagnold looks like Oscar?" Not what I saw of him, he didn't. Mischief's baby was a zillion times cuter.

Gram laughed. "No, silly! Like Spencer Tracy. I bet Ralph looked a lot like Spencer Tracy in his younger days."

"In whose younger days?" I asked, now thoroughly mixed up. "Ralph's or Spencer Tracy's?"

She sat down on the bed with me and studied her hands. "He actually held my hand tonight," she confided. "I haven't had a man hold my hand since your grandfather was alive."

I stared at her hands, too. There was nothing different about her familiar strong fingers and the brownish spots near her thumb. She rubbed the brown spots self-consciously. Then I noticed she was wearing pale pink nail polish. She never used to wear nail polish. I wondered if she'd borrowed some from my mother, but my mother never wore nail polish either. Somehow the sight of those pearly-pink nails filled me with a hollow uncertainty, as if everything I had ever known about Gram was no longer true. Almost as if I had made her up.

I touched her to make sure she was still there. That she was still my grandmother.

"Gram, I know about your secret," I blurted. "Mom does, too. We know you're dating that man." I deliberately didn't say his name. Once I gave him a name, he'd be real, too.

She threw back her head and laughed. "Lizzie, you should see your face! Have you become a judge and jury like your mother?"

"What do you mean?"

"First of all, it is no secret that I am dating Ralph Bagnold."

"How come you wouldn't tell me where you were going?" I demanded.

"I didn't realize I was keeping anything from you," Gram said sincerely. "I guess I've been distracted lately."

Maybe Gram hadn't meant to be secretive, but that didn't explain my mother's attitude. "Mom wouldn't tell me where you were either," I said.

Gram sighed. "I think your mother disapproves."

Trailing the belt of Gram's bathrobe across my lap so the kitten could play with it, I asked, "Why?"

"Lynn only met Ralph once," Gram said. I knew the conversation was getting serious when she used my mother's first name. Usually Gram refers to Mom as my mother or her daughter. "Ralph was as nice as could be, but Lynn treated him rather curtly, I thought. I was going to speak to her about her behavior but then I remembered that I did the very same thing to her when Lynn brought *her* boyfriends home."

"Is Mr. Bagnold your boyfriend?" I asked unbelievingly. It was bad enough Gram was dating, but a *boy*friend?

"She probably thinks he isn't good enough for me," Gram went on cheerfully. "I used to tell her the same thing. Isn't this rich? Mother and daughter, going full circle."

My head was going in a circle. This whole situation was too complicated for me. It was hard enough to picture my own mother having a boyfriend, much less my grandmother!

Since Gram was treating me like a grown-up, I struggled to make sense of what she was saying. "Do you think Mom is getting back at you for not liking her boyfriends?"

Gram thought that was funny. "No, dear, I don't believe your mother would carry a grudge that long. Anyway, I finally approved of one of her boyfriends. Your father."

"Has Dad met Mr. Bagnold?"

"Not yet," she replied. "I've been hoping to have Ralph over for dinner, but. . . ." She left the sentence unfinished. Obviously my mother wasn't anxious to get chummy with Mr. Bagnold.

"You'll like Ralph," Gram said. "He plays the piano, just like you do."

"The piano is dumb," I said sourly, slumping back on the pillows. "I'm thinking of switching to guitar." I wasn't, really. I just didn't want to have anything in common with Gram's date.

"Isn't this rather sudden, Lizzie?" She raised an eyebrow at me. "You've been taking piano lessons for years. And you're very good. It would be a shame to throw away all that training to learn a new instrument."

"I didn't say I was going to quit piano. I said I

was *thinking* about it." I softened my tone.

"Ralph is like your grandfather in many ways," she said.

Since my grandfather died before I was born, I only knew him through photographs and the stories Gram and Mom told. "Do you miss him?" I asked.

"Of course I miss him. Not a day goes by that I don't think of him."

"Then why are you going out with Mr. Bagnold?"

Gram took her time thinking of an answer. "It's nice to be around someone my age. Someone who understands that a good movie doesn't necessarily have a teenager in it. Things like that."

I felt vaguely insulted. I thought Gram liked going to the movies with me.

Fearfully I asked, "Gram, you and Mr. Bagnold aren't — going steady, are you?"

She laughed again. "Well," she answered, still chuckling. "I suppose you could say Mr. Bagnold and I are going steady. People who go steady only see one another. It's true Ralph and I aren't dating anyone else. But, Lizzie, it doesn't mean the same as when you kids go steady."

The bottom dropped out of my world.

Diary, can you imagine how I feel? *High school* kids go steady, not *grandmothers*! She said it didn't mean the same thing, but I'm not so sure.

Next Gram will come home with Ralph's class ring around her neck on a chain, if people in the olden days got class rings. Or she'll be wearing Ralph's burgundy jacket with the crest of their real estate agency on the pocket. When Josh started dating Jennifer Owens, he gave her his letter jacket. Jennifer wears it to school even though it's miles too big for her. Gram will probably be just as bad.

Diary, I can't let *any*body find out about my grandmother. I would just *die* of humiliation. Maybe she and Mr. Bagnold will have a fight or something and break up. Or maybe the whole thing will "blow over," as Dad said when Adam had that crush on his French teacher. In the meantime, though, I hope Gram and That Man stay out of public places.

The only good thing about this day was Mr. Rice's class. News of our one-day Read-A-Thon had spread, and our project was getting a lot of attention. Mr. Rice even came up with a slogan, "Read for Charity." Howie Strauch announced that his mother, who is a photographer, would take pictures that day. The pictures will be in the *Hampton Point Marketplace* — one of those free weekly newspapers people throw away — but still, it's publicity.

"Won't that be a dumb picture," Nancy commented, scowling. "A bunch of kids sitting around reading books. About as interesting as watching grass grow."

"At least we'll be famous, a little," I said. "It's not every day somebody comes to take our picture for a newpaper."

"I still think it's dumb." Nancy raised her hand. When Mr. Rice called on her, she said, "Howie's mother will just be wasting her time taking our picture. Why don't you tell her to take pictures of Mr. Devon's car wash? Or Miss Tyler's bake sale?"

Howie spoke up. "Look, Underpeace, you can't tell my mother what to do. You don't have to be in the picture. You'd probably break the camera anyway."

Nancy's face got red. "I wouldn't be in your mother's dumb picture if you begged me!"

"Fat chance," Howie returned.

Mr. Rice told them both to stop it. "No need to get excited, Nancy. December twentieth is still weeks away. If you're camera-shy, I'm sure we can arrange for you not to be in the photograph."

Then he went on to describe the book-cart he

planned to have in the classroom the day of our Read-A-Thon. During a regular library period, we'll pick out the books we'd like to read. The librarian will put all our books on a cart and roll it to our room, so we'll have our own personal library for the Read-A-Thon.

I barely listened to the teacher. I was more concerned about Nancy. She didn't usually act up in class, unless she had to read aloud and then she kidded around sometimes. I couldn't believe she really didn't want her picture in the newspaper. Something else must be bothering her.

"What is wrong with you?" I whispered. "Is it your father? Are you still having problems with him?"

"I haven't even seen him for two weeks," Nancy said. "He went to California on business and didn't get back until Monday."

"He was out of town? But I thought you went to see him last Wednesday," I said. "I tried to call you but your mother said you were out."

"How could I have gone to see him if he was in California?" Nancy was still irritated over her argument with Howie Strauch.

"Well, excuuuuuse me." Being best friends with Nancy is a real trial lately. She won't help me get revenge on Samantha Howard, even though she claims she hates Samantha as much as I do. She has all these mysterious appointments she won't tell me about. She doesn't want to have her picture in the newspaper. And she doesn't want to go with me to sign up pledges for the Read-A-Thon.

Suddenly I experienced the same weird feeling I had had in Gram's apartment. When Gram was talking about her date with Mr. Bagnold, I wasn't sure if I was listening to my grandmother or a stranger. Now I had that same feeling about Nancy.

I decided to give her another chance, for friendship's sake. "Nance, we've had our pledge sheets for days and we still haven't signed anybody up yet." That wasn't quite true — I had signed up my family yesterday. "Do you want to come with me this afternoon after school?"

I knew what she was going to say before the words were out of her mouth.

Sure enough, she said, "I can't." But then she surprised me with her next sentence. "How about this Saturday instead?"

"I have my piano lesson."

Nancy suddenly got angry. "Why do you always make everything so difficult, Lizzie Miletti?"

"Me! You're the one who can't go with me this afternoon. You know I have piano lessons on Saturday mornings." What was *with* her? "So we'll go after I get back. Why don't you come over around twelve and we'll have lunch first. Okay?"

"Okay," she said grudgingly.

"Don't let me twist your arm," I couldn't resist adding.

Our friendship seems so one-sided these days. I'm making *all* the effort and Nancy isn't making any. In fact, she acts as though she doesn't care if we are friends or not.

Sitting in the classroom, I fooled with a strand of my frizzy hair, thinking not very friendly thoughts. Nancy is definitely not ready to grow up yet, but I'm willing to wait for her (okay, so I'm not so sure *I'm* ready either). Plus I helped her when she was having problems with her father. I even went with her to Detroit one weekend to visit him. I suggested that she talk to him, let him know she didn't need to be entertained every second.

But what has Nancy done for me? She *did* help me pass a crucial history test a few weeks ago. I would have flunked otherwise. I thought we'd patched things up after the *disastrous* slumber party and our fight. And I thought we were united on our decision to get revenge on Samantha Howard. But look at how she's acting now! Maybe I don't know Nancy Underpeace very well at all.

I looked down and saw a sheet of paper under Nancy's desk. She was stepping all over it.

"You dropped something," I said, bending down to slide it out from under her shoe. "It's your sign-up sheet. You got it filthy."

Nancy snatched the pledge sheet from me. "Thanks," she said, but she didn't sound the least bit thankful.

Diary, nothing much happened to write about until today, Saturday.

I went to my piano lesson as usual. Nancy was supposed to come over at noon. We'd planned to eat lunch before we went around the neighborhood.

When I got home, Mom was making tuna fish sandwiches.

"Is Nancy here?" I asked breathlessly. I'd pedaled my bike top-speed all the way from my piano teacher's house.

"Upstairs with Gram. She's been up there over an hour," Mom remarked.

I was astonished. Nancy, who'd been acting like she was doing me a favor to say hello lately, had spent practically the whole morning with my grandmother!

Running up the steps, I could hear Nancy and Gram chattering away a mile a minute. As I walked into Gram's apartment, though, they both clammed up. Obviously they didn't want me to know what they were talking about.

I was plenty mad. Not jealous, because Nancy and Gram have always been friends and often get together to have a gab-fest. But neither of them had given me the time of day lately and now they shut me out of their little private conversation.

"I hope I'm not interrupting anything," I said loudly. "Mom has lunch ready. I want to get started before everyone goes out for the afternoon. You know how busy people are on Saturdays."

Nancy slid off Gram's bed. "I'm starved. Your mom makes the best tuna fish salad." She scooped her purse off a chair. "Oh, Lizzie, I just remembered something."

"What?"

"My sign-up sheet. I left it at home."

I felt like an overheated furnace. I was steaming! Signing pledges was the whole purpose of her coming over! "You won't need your sheet," I said, trying not to lose my temper. "You can write yours down on a plain piece of paper and then copy the names on your sheet when you get home."

Nancy looked disappointed. "I suppose I could," she said without enthusiasm. She waved to Gram. "Bye. Thanks for everything."

"Come back and see me again, Nancy," Gram

said. They looked at each other meaningfully, as if they shared a secret.

"Yeah, Nancy," I said sarcastically. "Don't be a stranger." I didn't know who made me the maddest — Nancy or my grandmother.

"What's eating you?" Nancy said as we left the room.

"Nothing, nothing at all," I replied airily. If Nancy didn't want to tell me her big secret, I wasn't about to beg her.

As I followed Nancy down the steps, I saw a paper sticking out of her purse. Her sign-up sheet! She had it with her all along!

Why would Nancy lie about not having her sign-up sheet? And *what* was she talking to Gram about?

I can't stand it, Diary. *More* secrets. I hate being on the outside of things. I remember this girl in my third-grade class who always whispered to her friend. The girl looked at me the whole time she whispered, so I knew she was talking about me. I'd go crazy trying to figure out what she was saying about me. Was my barrette crooked? Did I have a hole in my shirt? I've never liked secrets.

And now my two best friends in the world are keeping secrets from me.

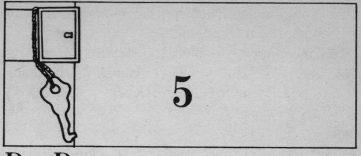

**5**

**D**ear **D**iary:

The absolute *worst* has happened! *Every*one in Claremont School knows about my grandmother!

Who do you think blabbed? Samantha Howard, that's who!

I can barely stand to *think* about what happened today, much less write about it. But here goes.

At lunch Nancy and Ericka Powell and I took our trays over to a table near where Samantha was holding court with her friends, Candace and Jessica. A few boys were sitting with them, too, drippy Donald Harrington and Robert Wilkins, who is a brain and ought to know better. I mean, if I were Robert, I'd worry about Donald's and Samantha's low IQ's rubbing off.

They were all talking, or rather Samantha was, and nobody paid any attention to us until we sat down.

Donald zinged his straw wrapper at me. Because he's a jerk, he does juvie stuff like that all the time. The wrapper landed right in my tapioca, which is hard enough to eat with all those tiny little things in it like fish eyes, without having Donald's grubby old straw wrapper on top.

"Yuck," Ericka commented. She's new to our school this year — she used to live in Alaska. Ericka is neat. She thinks Donald Harrington is a creep, too.

I flicked the wrapper off my tray. "Thanks a lot," I told Donald coldly. I was determined to remain in control. Donald Harrington was not going to rattle me.

Nancy zinged her straw wrapper right back at Donald. She has a good aim — hit him right between the eyes. "Gotcha!" she cried.

Donald picked up his dish of tapioca and made like he was going to throw it at us. I squealed and ducked, thinking we were in for a food fight. Donald was only bluffing. But during those few seconds, he wasn't listening to Queen Samantha or paying any attention to her.

And Samantha can't stand to be ignored even for a second. "Look who has a crush on Lizzie!" she sneered. "Honestly, Donald, I thought you had better taste." Candace and Jessica laughed like donkeys.

Of course Donald didn't want it spread all over school that he liked me (and neither did I!), so he pretended to hurl his dish of pudding at Robert instead, to save face.

But it was too late. "I suppose Donald and Lizzie will be going together soon, like somebody *else* I know," Samantha said slyly.

Jessica chanted, "Donald and Lizzie, sitting in a tree, k-i-s-s-i-n-g. First comes love, then comes marriage, then comes Donald pushing a baby — "

"Shut up!" Donald yelled.

Keeping my back turned, I tried to eat my lunch. Control, I told myself. Stay in control. If Samantha didn't have an audience, she'd shut up. But Donald's stupid stunt egged her on.

"Defending your true love," Samantha exclaimed. "How romantic."

"I don't even like Lizzie Miletti," Donald denied hotly. "I wouldn't like her if she was the last girl on earth. I wouldn't like her if she was the last girl in the entire universe — "

"That makes two of us!" I yelled back.

Samantha barreled on, over Donald's protest of how he wouldn't like me if I was the last person alive in whatever was bigger than the universe. "I wouldn't be surprised to see Donald and Lizzie holding hands coming out of Bentley's. Just the way I saw her grandmother and some strange *man*."

My fork clattered to the floor. I didn't pick it up — I was too stunned.

Ericka handed me her spoon, but I suddenly lost my appetite . . . and my control.

"Samantha's delirious," Nancy said. "She doesn't know what she's talking about."

But she did. And I knew what was coming next. Samantha was in complete control of the situation now.

"What about Lizzie's grandmother?" Jessica asked.

Samantha leaned forward as if to whisper, but everybody in two counties could have heard her. "It was the grossest thing. I was going into Bentley's to get an ice cream and these two old people were coming out. They were *holding hands* and looking at each other all gooey. One of them was Lizzie's grandmother!"

"Shut up!" Nancy shouted, but Samantha kept on.

"Can you *imagine*?" she shrieked. "Holding hands! At their age! If it had been *my* grandmother, I would have died on the spot."

Jessica put her two cents worth in. "They probably had an ice-cream soda with two straws."

"I didn't think old people *did* stuff like that," said Candace. "I mean, aren't they too old?"

Robert Wilkins came to my rescue.

When he spoke, I got up enough nerve to turn around. He glared at Candace over his glasses as he said, "I know you're going to find this hard to believe, but older people have feelings and emotions, too. It is perfectly possible for a mature person" — he emphasized the word "mature" — "to have a meaningful relationship, even someone our grandparents' age."

Samantha flipped her hair over her shoulder. "Oh, Robert. As usual, you've completely missed the point. Would you want *your* grandmother running around in public holding hands and looking all gooey-eyed at some old man? If *I* were Lizzie, I'd be terribly embarrassed."

I was. I was embarrassed enough when I found out about Gram and Mr. Bagnold, and I was a hundred times more embarrassed now that everybody else knew. Robert had tried, but Samantha scored a big one.

Ericka launched into a funny story about a camping trip in Alaska, but I scarcely heard a word. I knew she was trying to make me feel better. Only Samantha's transfer to another planet would make me feel better.

"Don't pay any attention to what Samantha said," Nancy advised as we took our trays up to the trash bins.

"But it's true," I cried. "Gram *is* running all over town with this man. His name is Ralph Bagnold."

"I know," Nancy said mildly. "She told me about him Saturday when I was over at your house. He sounds very nice. What's wrong with that?"

"What's wrong is the way they're acting! Like they're high school kids or something. It's — " I racked my brain for the right word. "It's *undignified* for Gram to be carrying on."

Nancy stared at me. "You're as bad as Samantha. You should be glad your grandmother found somebody her own age she likes. Did you ever think she might be lonely?"

"How could she be lonely? She has us — her whole family." It's technically impossible for anyone to be lonely in our house. There are too many people, too many animals, and too much is going on all the time. "She doesn't need that Ralph person. She has us," I repeated.

"Maybe that's not enough," Nancy said, leading the way out of the cafeteria.

"Whose side are you on?" I sputtered. I wasn't making much sense, but Samantha's scene had absolutely *ruined* my day.

I couldn't let her get away with it, either. It was time Miss Samantha Howard received another note from her secret admirer. I decided to speed up my plan. I wanted to see Samantha humiliated publicly, the way she had humiliated me.

I didn't get a chance to write Samantha's next note until the night before Thanksgiving. I had the entire Thanksgiving vacation, but I wanted to work on the note as soon as I had a few free hours. This time I would deliver the letter to Samantha's house, which was right around the corner from ours. I knew her family went away over the holidays, so no one would see me slip the note into their mailbox.

Delivering the note to her house also served another purpose — it told Samantha that her secret admirer probably lived in the neighborhood, another sign pointing to Adam. In the next note, I'd leave a stronger clue. The final note would be the kicker. And I would have the last laugh.

After I wrote the note and copied it over in my best imitation-Adam handwriting, I went downstairs.

In the kitchen Mom was chopping celery and onion for the chestnut stuffing. Darcy was polishing the silver, getting more pink cleaner on herself than on the knives and forks. Baby Rose nibbled celery as fast as Mom diced it.

"About time you showed up," Mom said testily.

"Give Darcy a hand with the silver. The forks are too hard for her to do."

I sat down with a polishing rag. "Where are the boys?"

"With your father, picking out the football games they intend to watch after dinner tomorrow." Mom blew a piece of hair upward out of her eyes. Her cheeks were flushed. Thanksgiving is a big deal in our house and a lot of work for my mother. She tends to get flustered easily. You'd think having been a nurse once would have taught her how to remain calm in an emergency.

But everyone always pitches in, even Rose, who will probably be assigned the job of shooing Sebastian and the cats away from the turkey until we actually eat. Darcy and I will set the table after Adam puts the extra leaf in it, and Josh will be in charge of the fire in the fireplace. Dad will make his special before-dinner cranberry punch and carve the bird. And Gram, of course, will help with the cooking. In fact, the chestnut stuffing is usually her territory.

"Where's Gram?" I asked Mom. "Don't tell me she has a *date* tonight."

"At the hairdresser's," Mom replied. "She worked today, but managed to get an appointment at the last minute. She wants to look extra-nice for tomorrow."

I finished the forks and started on the spoons. Darcy was still working on the knives. I decided to tell Gram friend-to-friend, as soon as she came in, that she ought to cool it with Mr. Bagnold, at least while they were in public, where other people could see them. It's been a long time since Gram went out, and she'd probably be grateful for the tip.

"I wish I could go to the hairdresser's," Mom said. "I won't even have time to comb my hair tomorrow, much less have it styled."

"Why are you knocking yourself out? Gram will be back soon. She'll help cook like she always does."

My mother slammed a drawer. "She won't be here tomorrow."

I thought my mother was joking. "Of course she'll be here. Where else would she go? It's Thanksgiving."

Darcy piped up importantly, "She's going to eat with Mr. Bagnold's family."

"What?" The polishing rag slipped from my fingers. I seemed to be dropping things a lot. One look at my mother's face told me Darcy wasn't kidding.

"It's true," Mom said. "Mr. Bagnold's daughter called Gram this morning and invited her to eat with their family. She doesn't live too far from here, apparently."

I still couldn't believe it. "She can't do that! Gram always eats with us. We're her family! It's — tradition! She can't break tradition."

"Lizzie," Mom said patiently. "My mother is a grown woman. She can eat Thanksgiving dinner wherever and with whomever she pleases."

"And you don't mind?"

"Of course I mind, but I'm not my mother's keeper. Gram lives with us because she wants to and we want her here. But she's still her own person. I can't treat my mother like one of my children." Mom spoke crisply but I could tell she wasn't happy with Gram's sudden change in plans. Quickly she scraped diced celery and onion off the cutting board into a plastic bag and tied it with a twistee.

Darcy, who for once in her life hadn't pestered us with a million questions, suddenly caught the gist of our conversation. "You mean, Gram's not going to be here for dinner *at all*?"

With her head in the depths of the refrigerator, Mom replied, "Well, not for the main part of our dinner. She and Mr. Bagnold will drop by later for coffee and dessert."

"Whose idea was that?" I wanted to know.

"Gram's."

Coffee and dessert! That sounded awfully formal. The only person who ever comes to our house for coffee and dessert is Dad's boss. We sit around the living room like statues, dressed-up and polite, while Darcy passes around a plate of nut bread. Everybody breathes a sigh of relief when the royal visit is over. And now Gram is bringing her boyfriend for all of us to meet the same way.

"Maybe he'll bring us a present," Darcy said hopefully.

"Don't bet on it," I said, angry that my sister could be bought so easily.

"Dad's boss brought us a box of candy," Darcy said.

I remembered. All dark, bitter chocolates. At least it wasn't some dreadful Roth Frozen Food product. I would rather have had a Hershey bar. But even if Mr. Bagnold came with a whole truckload of Hershey bars, I wouldn't care.

Thanksgiving dinner was awful.

Mom tried hard, so nobody could complain about the food. The turkey was terrific, but the dressing wasn't quite as good as it usually was. Neither was the sweet-potato casserole. Gram usually cooks those dishes. When she came in last night, her hair in swirls, she offered to stay up

68

and make them, but Mom told her shortly that it wasn't necessary.

That was really all they said to each other. Gram went up to her room and watched television. I didn't go up to see her either.

This morning, Gram came downstairs in a blue dress I hadn't seen before. I didn't say anything about how she looked. Mom was a little cool to her, too, I noticed. Gram looked almost sad, as if she was trying not to cry. But then the doorbell rang and she hurried to get her coat. Mr. Bagnold took her away in his big blue car.

Darcy, Rose, and I watched the Macy's parade on television. Normally I love the parade, but today it seemed to go on forever before we finally saw Santa Claus. Rose can't bear to miss even a single glimpse of Santa Claus. She squealed when she saw him and ran over to kiss the television screen. Darcy thought that was very funny. She knows there isn't any Santa Claus and acts a little superior around Rose. Mom warned Darcy — and all of us kids — not to spoil it for Rose. "She'll find out the truth soon enough," she said. "Let her enjoy the magic while she can." I thought the magic had certainly gone out of the day for the rest of us. And it was Gram's fault.

At one o'clock we sat down to dinner. I wasn't very hungry. Mom didn't have much appetite either. She kept looking over at Gram's empty place.

After dinner, Dad, Josh, and Adam cleaned up the kitchen and did the dishes (while watching a game on the portable TV). Mom collapsed in the recliner. Darcy and Rose went outside to play.

And I had an important errand to run.

"I'm going to walk Sebastian," I told Mom. Walking the dog wasn't my real errand. More like my cover.

I took the dog past Samantha's house. Making sure the coast was clear, I stuck the sealed envelope in her mailbox. Then I walked Sebastian past Nancy's house, but no one was home there either. Nancy and her mother had been invited to eat at a friend of her mother's, and then Nancy was going to her father's.

The neighborhood was quiet. I scuffed leaves on my way back home, feeling rotten. How could Gram do this, ruin one of the few perfect family holidays of the year? Didn't she care about us anymore?

Around seven that evening, I heard a clanky car engine. Gram and Mr. Bagnold had arrived for coffee and dessert.

I checked my reflection in the mirror over my dresser. I had changed from my good skirt and sweater to walk Sebastian so I was wearing jeans and a sweatshirt. I wasn't about to change back into good clothes just to meet That Man.

Dad opened the door for them, as if Gram were a guest and not a member of the family. They came inside, and drafts of cold air came with them.

Mr. Bagnold was a cheerful-looking man, now that I saw him up close. He had that stomach that made me think of a cookie jar, and gray hair combed carefully to hide his bald spot. He helped Gram out of her coat, then stood still while she unwound a silk scarf from around her neck.

Gram's face was flushed. She looked very pretty in her new blue dress. They both laughed at something Dad said. It was plain that Mr. Bagnold liked Gram very much. And she liked him. She looked very happy.

But Mom didn't. Her smile was wavery. Pinned on, almost.

She went out to the kitchen to get the pie she had saved from dinner and to put the coffee on. Dad led Mr. Bagnold into the living room. Darcy and Rose tumbled around him like puppies, the little traitors. Even Adam and Josh shook Mr. Bagnold's hand.

"Lizzie!" Gram cried. "There you are! Ralph, I want you to meet my oldest granddaughter, Elizabeth. We call her Lizzie."

"How do you do?" Mr. Bagnold said to me, smiling. "Betty, she's the very image of you at that age, I bet."

Gram laughed. "Oh, Lizzie's a lot prettier than I ever was."

Why were they talking about the way I looked? I'm not really pretty, not with my frizzy brown hair. I hated Gram's tone, like I was some neighbor's kid and not her favorite grandchild.

They sat down on the sofa. Gram patted the cushion next to her. "Lizzie, come sit here. I want Ralph to get to know my family."

"I can't," I blurted. "I have to go help Mom." I ran from the room before Gram could stop me.

Instead of going into the kitchen, I flew upstairs into my own room. I know, Diary, I blew my promise to act like I'm in control of my life. The article in Mom's magazine said to avoid getting unduly upset over things. And let's face it — running out like that was not the act of a person in control of her life. I couldn't help it, Diary, I just couldn't bear to see them together.

I probably shouldn't write this where somebody might read it, but I'm not sure about Gram anymore. She can't belong to two families. Either she's with the Milettis or she's not.

If she was forced to choose, I wonder who Gram would pick — us . . . or That Man.

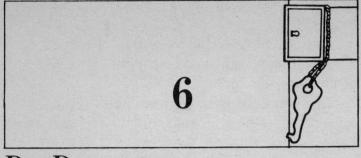

# 6

**D**ear **D**iary:

I went shopping today with Nancy.

Nancy was home from her father's and Mom drove us to the mall. We split up in front of the fountain, promising my mother we'd meet her there at two-thirty.

As soon as Nancy and I were alone, I mentioned my Thanksgiving mission. We hadn't talked since school ended for the holiday.

"Guess what?" I said. "Samantha got her second love letter from her secret admirer."

"How?" Nancy asked.

"I put it in her mailbox Thursday, while everyone was away."

"Clever," she said approvingly.

I did a little dance. "I can't wait to go back to school Monday and see if she fell for it again."

"I can wait," Nancy said. "School is a drag. The weekends aren't long enough."

"How come you didn't stay at your dad's longer?"

"He had another business trip. I stayed with him Thursday night and last night, so it was sort of like a weekend."

"Are you getting along with him better?" I inquired. "Or is he still wearing you out with a million activities?"

"Not really. Dad is so tired from these trips he's been taking lately, we've been spending more time at his apartment. This time we rented movies. I made popcorn and that was our supper. After all that turkey, junk food tasted great."

We walked along slowly, glad to be together again. The mall was getting more crowded by the minute. Some woman accidentally ran a stroller over my foot. She apologized, but my toes hurt like crazy.

"We're still eating turkey," I said, rubbing my foot. "We'll have it every meal but breakfast till the last crumb is gone."

"I wish we could have had a big family dinner like you did," Nancy said wistfully. "It was okay at my mom's friend's house, but it wasn't like those people were family or anything. At least it was an improvement over last year. Mom and I ate in a restaurant and then I went to Dad's and *he* took me to a restaurant."

"I remember. My folks invited you guys to our house," I said.

"Mom thought it would be better if we got away by ourselves. So we could talk." Holidays are always rough for Nancy.

"Well, you wouldn't have had fun at our house this year," I told her. "With Gram not there, it was horrible. My mother hardly said a word. And then Gram and That Man came later to have dessert."

"What's he like?" Nancy asked.

"I don't know. I didn't stick around. I'm mad at Gram. It's her fault our family isn't like it was before," I said bitterly. "She's changing."

Nancy stared at me. "I don't believe you, Lizzie Miletti. You act like your grandmother committed a crime or something. She hasn't changed."

"Yes, she has," I insisted. "She's just like Josh now. He bought every tape U2 ever made, just because Jennifer Owens likes U2. And he can't stand the group."

"What does that have to do with your grandmother?"

"Gram is doing the same thing," I explained. "Josh is changing to please Jennifer and Gram is changing to please That Man. She never wore black shoes before she met Ralph Bagnold. She hates black shoes." I didn't really care what color shoes Gram wore — I was upset because she chose Mr. Bagnold over us, her own family.

Nancy shook her head. "I think you're nuts. Your grandmother is the same person."

Deep down inside, I hoped Nancy was right. But that didn't make the hurt go away, any more than the woman's apology for running over my toes made my foot feel better.

We stopped in front of a window showing party dresses.

"Look at that dress!" I cried. "Isn't it gorgeous? I'd love to have a dress like that." The dress had a black velvet top and a full red skirt of some silky material.

"You're too young," Nancy said matter-of-factly. "Where would you wear a dress that fancy?"

"To a dance, maybe." I wished I had enough nerve to try it on. I was dying to twirl in that silky red skirt.

"Dream on." Nancy turned from the display to sit on a marble ledge.

I stared longingly at the dress a few more seconds, then joined Nancy on the ledge.

"You know," I said. "We might have a dance later this year. The sixth-graders, I mean. I heard Samantha and some of the other girls talking about it."

"Samantha." Nancy made a face. "Who else would want a dance? I'm surprised the Queen doesn't want to have a ball. I'd rather have a pizza party, myself."

I'm not too sure, Diary, how I feel about a sixth-grade dance. The idea sort of scares me. It's kind of like that fancy dress. In a way I wanted to try it on, but I was afraid I'd look dumb in it. At the dance, we'd have to *dance*. With *boys*. I'd even be afraid to dance with Billy Watts (not that he'd ever ask me).

"Are you hungry?" Nancy asked. She had forgotten about the dance. "Want to split an order of fries?"

"Okay."

As we stood up, I saw a couple from our neighborhood. "Hey, isn't that Mr. and Mrs. Dunbar, from around the corner?"

Nancy squinted in the direction I pointed in. "Yeah. So what? We'll probably see a lot of people we know here today. I think everybody in the world is in this mall."

I fished my Read-A-Thon sign-up sheet from my purse. I carried it with me at all times, just in case. "They weren't home the day we went around signing up pledges," I said. "Now's our chance. Come on."

Nancy held me back. "Our chance to do what?"

"Sign them up for the Read-A-Thon, what else?" Sometimes Nancy acted so *dense*.

"I don't have my sheet with me," she said.

So what else was new? Nancy never had her pledge sheet with her. She might as well fold it into a paper airplane and sail it out the window.

"We'll ask them to sign the back of mine," I suggested impatiently. "And we'll put a note on yours. I'm sure Mr. Rice will accept two signatures, one for me and one for you. Come on, before we lose them in this mob."

Reluctantly, Nancy trailed me across the mall. For some crazy reason, she hid behind this huge fake tree, while I went into my famous, never-fail pitch. No one ever refused to pledge, especially after they heard it was for such a good cause.

"Of course we'll contribute," Mrs. Dunbar agreed, scanning the sign-up sheet. "I see your goal is to read seventy-five pages. I'm sure you can do it. Put me down for the full amount."

"Ten dollars? Great. If I only read fifty pages, you only have to pay five dollars," I told her. "One dollar for every ten pages I actually read. Mr. Rice hopes we'll raise a lot of money for Children's Hospital."

"I think it's wonderful," Mrs. Dunbar said. Then she noticed Nancy half-hidden behind the tree. "What about you, Nancy? Aren't you in Lizzie's class?"

Nancy ducked back behind the tree. I could have killed her! She was about to blow ten dollars for Children's Hospital.

"Yes, she is," I answered quickly, before the Dunbars changed their minds. "She forgot her pledge sheet, but she'd love it if you pledged for her, too. You can sign the back of mine, if you want."

Nancy sidled over. "You don't have to pledge. I have loads of signatures." She did? This was news to me.

"Don't be silly." Mrs. Dunbar signed the back of my pledge sheet. "I want to support both you girls. The world needs more young people like you two."

"Well, don't pledge very much," Nancy said nervously. "A dollar is fine. Or even fifty cents."

I elbowed her in the ribs. "Are you out of your mind?" I said under my breath. "What are you trying to do — scare off customers?"

Mrs. Dunbar gave the sheet back to me. As I thanked her, I noticed the amount she had jotted down.

"Ten dollars for seventy-five pages!" I exclaimed when Mr. and Mrs. Dunbar wandered off.

"She pledged the same as mine! Isn't that terrific, Nancy?"

Nancy's face was pale, as if she were coming down with the flu. Or she had just received terrible news.

That's what I mean about not understanding Nancy anymore, Diary. We both just earned twenty dollars for Children's Hospital (or we would after the Read-A-Thon), and Nancy acted like it was the worst thing in the world.

Our shopping trip went downhill from there. Nancy didn't say much, and she didn't buy anything either. I bought a Christmas present, a book for Darcy — one of those question-and-answer encylopedias.

Nancy glanced at it scornfully. "A book? What kind of a present is that to give a little kid?"

"Darcy will love it," I said, defending my purchase. "It's got pictures of Charlie Brown and Snoopy. Plus it has answers to the questions she's always asking, like where does the sun go at night."

"I still think she'd rather have something else. Something fun. I know *I* wouldn't want a book for a present."

We met Mom at the fountain and went home. I didn't talk to Nancy the rest of the weekend.

Usually we call each other every night. I dialed her house on Sunday evening but there wasn't any answer. I figured she was out with her mother.

Monday we went back to school. I was anxious to see how Samantha reacted to her second love letter. Knowing Samantha, she'd probably brag about her "love letter" to her friends.

I was right.

Candace Quinn and Jessica Aldridge were clustered around Samantha's desk when I walked into the classroom. They were giggling and whispering. As I went by I caught a glimpse of the letter I had written. Samantha was so excited, her face glowed. She'd fallen for my joke *again*.

Nancy came in a few minutes later, still puffing from her bike ride.

"What's with Her Majesty?" she asked as she sat down and unloaded her knapsack.

"It's my letter. I told you I put it in her mailbox, remember?"

"Well, it looks like your plan is working. Samantha's practically foaming at the mouth. I guess she really believes some guy is in love with her." Nancy stowed her lunch under her desk.

"The last note will be the best," I said confidently. "Her secret admirer will set up a meeting. He won't show up because he doesn't exist! I'll have the last laugh."

"You might have the last laugh, but Samantha won't know who set her up," Nancy pointed out. "She'll just forget about it and go right back to being her snobby self again."

I hadn't thought of that. It wouldn't be revenge if Samantha didn't *know* I made up the whole thing. Somehow I would have to be there when Samantha was stood up by her secret admirer.

After lunch today, our class went to the library to pick out books for the Read-A-Thon. The big event was less than three weeks away.

"Choose three books you'd like to read that day," Mr. Rice told us. "Make sure they are interesting. You'll be spending the entire day reading, and you won't want to be stuck with a boring book."

"All books are boring," Nancy muttered under her breath.

Mr. Rice continued. "When you've made your selection, take the books to Mrs. Hunt. You can check them out now, but Mrs. Hunt will set them aside until December twentieth. That way we'll be assured of having the books we want on that day. I'm going to add some of my own favorites, in case we don't have enough books. We wouldn't want to run out of reading material!"

Nancy rolled her eyes. "Heaven forbid."

I knew exactly which books I wanted and went

straight for them. A Nancy Drew I hadn't read, *Little Women*, and a book about a cat that walked a hundred miles to find its family.

Nancy thumbed carelessly through *Little Women*. "You're going to read all these in one day?"

"Maybe not all of them," I replied. "I'll probably switch back and forth. Now let's go find your books."

We happened to be standing by the primary kids' books. Nancy reached out and plucked a book off the shelf. It was one of those itty-bitty Beatrix Potter books, *The Tale of Squirrel Nutkin*.

"Here's mine," she said.

I burst out laughing. "Honestly, Nancy. You are so funny! That book has all of twelve pages in it."

"Fifty-nine," Nancy said quietly.

"Yeah, but half of them are pictures! And there are only about two words on each page."

Abruptly she shoved the book back into the bookcase. "I guess you're right."

We wandered around the library. Nancy couldn't seem to find any books she liked. Most of the kids were already in the checkout line.

"Can't you find *any*thing?" I asked wearily. "I mean, the whole library is filled with books. Surely there must be something here."

At last Nancy pulled a big thick book from the science shelf. "I'll take this one," she said firmly. "And that's it. This book should count as three."

"Are you sure you want that one?" I asked. "It looks hard." The book was about three inches thick, with lots of fine print and not many pictures. The only book in the library thicker than that science book was the dictionary.

"This is the one I want." Nancy lugged the book into the line.

Donald Harrington was in front of her. He wheeled around and glanced at the book she had picked.

"Hey, Underwear! You can't read that," he jeered. "You can barely read baby books!"

All the kids in the line giggled, including Samantha, who was checking out three skinny books on beauty and fashion.

"That's enough," Mr. Rice said sternly. "Donald, one more comment from you and you'll go to the office."

Mrs. Hunt stamped the card in Nancy's book. "I see you only have one book, but it's a lulu!" she said cheerfully. She put the science book in the stack with the others.

Then it was my turn. Before Mrs. Hunt finished stamping my books, Nancy came back. She had another book in her hand.

"I want this one, too," she said in a low voice. "Is that okay?"

Mrs. Hunt smiled at her. "Of course it's okay." The librarian put Nancy's new book in the pile, but not before I saw the title.

It was *The Tale of Squirrel Nutkin*. The baby book from the little kids' section.

Surely Nancy was kidding with that book. Then I decided she only chose it as a sort of protest against the Read-A-Thon. Reading that baby book was her way of letting Mr. Rice know she didn't like his project.

I really don't understand Nancy anymore. In some ways she acts so babyish, riding her bike to school and everything. But in other ways, she seems to say to the world, "Don't mess with me," like not going along with my revenge plan or Mr. Rice's Read-A-Thon.

I wish I had that much control over my own life.

**7**

**D**ear **D**iary:

Dad came home this evening with a Christmas tree. Nothing so bad about that, except that it is only the first *week* in December. He does this every year, buys the very first tree he sees. The needles will drop off by Christmas, and Mom will have a fit because the tree looks awful. Dad will have to go out and buy another tree. It happens every year.

Right now everybody except me is downstairs helping Dad put up the tree. Adam is playing his new Christmas album, with songs sung by rock stars. I can hear Josh teasing Sebastian, making him run and bark. Rose is shrieking that she *has* to place the angel on top of the tree.

I need peace and quiet, Diary. I have problems to think about, and I can't do it around a million people.

Here are my main problems:

1. Samantha — How to make her look like an idiot and let her know *I'm* the person who did it.

2. Gram — How to make her see she can't be in two families at once. She's with us or she isn't.

3. Nancy — Question mark. I know there is *some*thing wrong with Nancy but I can't put my finger on it. Some days she acts like my friend and some days she doesn't. Maybe our friendship is falling apart, after all these years. Maybe she just doesn't like me as much any more.

Rats! Somebody is knocking at my door. I can't have five seconds of privacy! Later, Diary . . .


Well, I'm back. That was Darcy, with a problem of her own.

She poked her head around the door and said, "Lizzie, I'm in trouble. Can I come in?"

I did not want to hear what awful thing my little sister had done. But she looked so pathetic, I couldn't refuse.

Dragging a paper sack, she sat down on my bed with the most forlorn expression I had ever seen.

"Darcy, what is it?" I asked. "It can't be that bad."

"Yes, it is." Her bottom lip quivered. Opening the sack, she took out a huge blue-and-white dish and two leather collars set with colored rhinestones.

I stared at the strange objects. "*What* are those?"

"Christmas presents. I bought them with the money Mom gave me." She handed me the blue-and-white china dish. "This is for Sebastian. It's a dog bowl for big dogs."

"It certainly is," I agreed. You could have floated a cruise ship in that dish. "Are those collars for Sebastian, too?"

"No, they're for Marilyn and Elvis. Aren't they pretty? The other cats in the neighborhood will be so jealous, 'cause ours will be wearing diamonds."

I fingered the "diamonds" on one of the collars. Elvis and Marilyn weren't likely to be thrilled with their presents, but, as the saying goes, it's the thought that counts.

"It was nice of you to think of Sebastian and the cats. Why is that so bad?"

Tears spilled down her cheeks. "I spent all my money!"

The price tags were still on the dish and collars. I added them up in my head. "These things only come to eight dollars," I said. "You should have two dollars left. Where's the rest of your money?"

"I put it in the bell man's pot," she sobbed.

"The bell man's pot? — oh, you mean the guy ringing the bell. The Salvation Army. Oh, Darcy." Now I understood.

Darcy had begged Mom to let her shop by herself. And when Mom let her, she spent her money on the cats and the dog and gave the rest to charity. Which means she didn't have any left to buy presents for the family.

"What am I going to do?" she wailed.

"Darcy, buying gifts for the animals isn't terrible. And giving money to needy people is very sweet."

"But how am I going to buy presents for Mom and Dad and you and Gram and her cats and everybody? Mom will be mad at me if she finds out."

"No, she won't," I said. "Why don't you talk to her?"

Still crying, Darcy shook her head. "Won't you help me, Lizzie?" she pleaded.

My first thought was to retreat back downstairs. I'm not any good at this. I don't know how to be the kind of big sister my little sisters can turn to in a crisis. I can't handle my *own* problems, much less Darcy's.

Wrapping my arms around her, I rested my chin on Darcy's head until she cried herself down to hiccups. We needed Gram. Gram would know what to do. But Gram was out with Mr. Bagnold, having dinner at the new Chinese restaurant in the mall.

I felt a stab of anger. Why wasn't she home with us, where she belonged? Gram was out practically all the time now, while her family did dumb things. Like Dad buying a tree way too early or Darcy wasting her money on foolish presents.

Music from Adam's album floated upstairs — Bruce Springsteen singing "Santa Claus Is Coming to Town." The words were familiar — we sang it in our school winter concert — but the music was all wrong. If Gram were here, she'd let Adam play a little of that record, then she'd put on her album, the one we listened to every year.

But Gram wasn't here.

And Darcy needed someone now.

"Okay," I said, sighing. "I'll help."

Darcy brightened. "Will you lend me some of your money?"

"I can't. I barely have enough as it is. But I have an idea. Something even better." I got up and went to my desk. Gathering paper, cardboard, markers, glue, and a tube of glitter, I dumped the items onto the bed.

"What do I do with this stuff?" Darcy asked, looking doubtfully at the pile of supplies.

"Make your own presents. Homemade presents

are nicer than store-bought ones any day."

"Nobody really likes homemade presents," she muttered.

I remembered how Gram would always give me a pep talk whenever I needed convincing. "Sure they do. Think about Laura and Ma and Pa on *Little House on the Prairie*. They didn't have any money for presents. They made all theirs."

Darcy considered the pile again. She loves the old TV shows that came on cable. I know shows like *The Brady Bunch* or *Little House on the Prairie* are just stories, but Darcy believes those programs are real.

"Mom puts all my drawings and good papers on the refrigerator," she said, starting to accept my idea.

"You can do a really terrific drawing for her," I said. "And make a frame for it out of cardboard. There are lots of things you can make." I picked up a piece of cardboard. "Here. I'll show you."

So instead of wrestling with my own problems, I spent the evening cutting pretty pictures from magazines for a calendar for Dad and gluing glitter-covered paper around an orange juice can for Josh's pencil holder.

In a way it was kind of fun. Fooling around with construction paper reminded me of all the tacky projects I made in first and second grade. Darcy didn't think the things we made were tacky. She was caught up pretending to be Laura Ingalls, happy to have homemade gifts for the people in her family and wonderful, grand gifts for the animals in her family. Life was simple for an eight-year-old.

By the time we put the glue and glitter away and picked up a million paper scraps, it was time for bed. I never got around to worrying about my list of troubles. Funny, but the list didn't seem quite so long anymore.

Good night, Diary.

# 8

**D**ear **D**iary:

I couldn't believe it! My whole plan to get even with Samantha practically blew up in my face. And you'll never guess who caused it.

Samantha! And Adam, my own brother!

After school Mom asked Adam to ride his bike to the 7/Eleven for a gallon of milk. I didn't have anything to do and it was a nice day, so I offered to go with him. I knew he would buy a bag of chips with the change and he'd need help eating them.

"You'd better keep up. I'm not waiting for you," he said, leaping on his bike and flying down the street. Nothing like brotherly love.

At the 7/Eleven we got Mom's milk, then argued over what kind of chips to buy with the change. Adam wanted sour cream and onion. I wanted rippled barbecue. It isn't often we have a chance to eat normal junk food. Since Dad brings home sample products from Roth Frozen Foods,

Mom refuses to buy chips or pretzels.

"Consider yourselves lucky," she tells us whenever we whine that there's nothing to eat in the house. "You have a variety of after-school snacks other kids would envy."

Not true. Nobody I know would ever envy a tray of piping-hot microwaved zucchini-and-pea sticks when they could have popcorn.

"Mom asked *me* to go to the store," Adam said, trying to settle the argument with his usual fairness. "I get to pick." He grabbed the package of sour cream and onion.

"Split with me?" I asked. With Adam you can't take anything for granted.

"Maybe." He strutted up to the counter.

As we rounded the corner I saw them. Samantha and Jessica. Samantha had the latest issue of *Seventeen* clutched in her hand.

"Hi, Samantha," I said flatly.

"Hi, Lizzie." She didn't even glance at me. She was grinning at Adam. "Hello, Adam." Her voice was like velvet. If she were a cat, she would have purred.

"Uh — hi," Adam replied uneasily. He suddenly became engrossed in the car and motorcycle magazines in the rack.

Samantha looked smashing, as always. She had

on slim khaki pants tucked into lace-up leather boots and an oversized red-and-brown sweater. Her long blonde hair fell down her back in a single thick braid tied with a leather thong. She could have stepped right out of the *Seventeen* she was holding.

Next to her I felt dumpy in my jeans and old sweatshirt. Of course, anyone but Princess Diana would feel dowdy next to Samantha.

"What a coincidence," Samantha practically cooed to Adam. "Running into you here. I was just on my way over to your house to see you."

"You were?" Adam asked incredulously.

"Yes, I was wondering if you'd like to sign my pledge sheet. You know, for the Read-A-Thon our class is having?"

I nearly went into orbit. "Samantha!" I exclaimed. "Adam already pledged to me and Nancy! My whole family has. You're wasting your breath."

Ignoring me, she asked Adam, "Are you sure you won't pledge? Even a dollar? Pretty please?"

Adam got so flustered he nearly dropped the milk. "I don't think so," he mumbled.

Samantha exchanged a quick look with Jessica. "Guess what? I'm learning handwriting analysis. It's really fascinating. You can find out all kinds of things about people by studying their hand-writing. Do you write letters, Adam?" she asked meaningfully.

"Huh?" Adam scratched his head.

Perspiration trickled down my spine. Samantha was hinting that she believed Adam was her se-cret admirer. Naturally Adam had no idea what she was talking about.

"Adam, we'd better get this milk home before it sours," I said hastily.

Samantha dug a little notepad from her purse. "Before you go, Adam, would you write your name on here? I need lots of samples to study if I'm ever going to be any good at analyzing hand-writing." She batted her eyelashes at him. "Your handwriting will reveal the *real* you."

My brain was clicking along at fifty miles an hour. What was Samantha's angle? First she wanted Adam to sign her pledge sheet and when he wouldn't do that, she asked him to sign a note-pad so she could analyze his handwriting. I didn't believe the handwriting analysis story for a sec-ond. She was up to something. Whatever it was, she needed Adam's signature. Was she planning to forge checks? Adam didn't have any money in the bank.

Then it struck me. Sly Samantha wanted Ad-am's signature to compare it with the handwriting in the letters I sent her. She must have decided that Adam was her secret admirer and now she wanted proof.

The notes I wrote to Samantha resembled Adam's handwriting, but not exactly. If she got his real signature and compared it with the letters, she'd know the letters were written by somebody else. Somebody playing a trick on her. That somebody was me, but I didn't want Samantha to find out before the Grand Finale. I had worked too hard to let my plan go up in a puff of smoke.

I could tell Adam was actually considering signing that paper.

I did the only thing I could think of. I sneezed. Not an ordinary sneeze, either, but a great, big WACHOO sneeze. The kind of sneeze that made people turn around and look.

"Yuck!" Samantha said in disgust, holding her magazine up like a shield.

"Sorry." I sniffled so they wouldn't think my sneeze was fake. "I'm coming down with a terrible cold. It's probably catching. I bet I'm loaded with germs."

Samantha whirled and stomped up to the checkout counter, eager to get away from me, the walking germ.

What a close call! I decided then and there to write the last note to Samantha and deliver it to

97

her soon. Before she figured out another way to get Adam's signature.

On Friday it snowed. Everybody was home, even Gram. Because the roads weren't plowed very well (although they were cleared well enough for the schools to stay open), Gram postponed her date with Mr. Bagnold.

After supper Mom and Gram started baking sugar cookies.

"I get to put on the sprinkles," Darcy cried.

"Me, too!" Rose chirped, not to be outdone.

"You can't sprinkle cookies and write to Santa Claus both," I told her. Rose had been working on her letter to Santa all week. She could only write her name, so I was helping her. It was taking us forever. I am getting to be an expert at writing letters from other people.

We were all sitting around the kitchen table like a real family, with the wonderful smell of sugar cookies in the air. Adam was playing Gram's record of carols. We looked like a scene from a greeting card.

Gram will realize what she's missing and come back to us, I thought, as I guided Rose's hand to make an S. The holidays do that, make people come together. At least, that's what everyone says.

"I think I'll have both a turkey and a ham this year," Mom was saying to Gram. "The ham for Christmas Eve and the turkey for dinner Christmas Day. What do you think?"

Gram slid the next batch of cookies into the oven. When she stood, her face was serious. "I can't put it off any longer," she confessed.

"Put what off?" Mom asked mildly.

"Lynn, I won't be here for Christmas. Ralph and I have made plans to visit friends upstate. We'll go antiquing and have dinner at this lovely old lodge — "

Mom stared at Gram, speechless.

"Not be here with us!" I yelled, nearly ruining Rose's letter. "Gram! It's Christmas!"

"I know, Lizzie." Gram glanced at Rose and Darcy. "Angels," she said to them. "Would you mind telling Adam to play the other side of the record?"

After Darcy and Rose left the room, Gram said, "I know it's Christmas. This is the hardest decision I've ever had to make. Ralph and I talked it over. If we spend Christmas here with you, then his children will be hurt, and if we spend Christmas with his children, then you and Bob will feel left out. . . ."

"Why don't you divide your time?" Mom suggested. "Spend Christmas Eve with us and

Christmas Day with Ralph's family."

I hated the idea. "No! She has to be here Christmas Day, too."

Gram looked helplessly at Mom. "See? See what happens when we try to compromise? It would be the same with Ralph's family. This is the only solution, Lynn. If we go someplace neutral, no one will have their feelings ruffled. You understand, don't you?"

Mom sliced the roll of cookie dough with blunt motions. "Do what you want," she said stiffly. "Don't worry about us."

"I knew this was going to happen," Gram said miserably. "I just knew it. I almost wish — " She broke off, untying the dish towel she wore as an apron.

"You wish what, Gram?" I pressed. "That you didn't have to go with Mr. Bagnold? You don't, really. Just tell him you want to spend Christmas with your family. Like you always have."

Gram brushed past me. I could see tears in her eyes. "Please don't make this harder than it is, Lizzie."

"You're the one making it hard!" I called after her.

"Lizzie." Mom spoke sharply. "Don't talk to your grandmother that way. Go apologize to her."

"Apologize! She's the one who's leaving and *I* have to apologize?" The perfect greeting-card scene was shattered. Everything was wrong.

Nancy came over late to visit her kitten. I wasn't in the mood for company. Not even my best friend.

We went up to my room. Nancy sprawled on the floor, dangling a scrap of string for Oscar to play with.

"Your grandmother seems to think I can take him home in a couple of weeks," she said. The kitten skittered back and forth, chasing the string.

"When did she say that?" I was adding up my pledges for the Read-A-Thon. So far four people had signed up for the full amount, ten dollars. If I read seventy-five pages, I'd collect forty dollars for Children's Hospital.

"Yesterday. I saw her at the mailbox. Ouch!" Oscar got carried away and pounced on Nancy's hand. "This cat's claws are sharp!"

"You'll never guess what Gram told us tonight," I announced. "She's not spending Christmas with us."

"I know," Nancy said. "She and Mr. Bagnold are going to see some friends."

I threw down my pencil. "She told you that

101

yesterday?" I was practically shouting. I couldn't help it. "She just informed *us* tonight. I guess she couldn't be bothered to tell her own family."

Nancy stared at me. "Are you mad because your grandmother told me first?"

I was, but I didn't want to admit it. Obviously Gram and Nancy still had their little secrets. I changed the subject completely.

"How many signatures do you have on your sign-up sheet?" I asked.

"Why?" Nancy was suspicious. "Are you taking a survey?"

"I'm just *asking*, Nancy. Why are you so touchy about the Read-A-Thon?"

"Why are you so nosy?" she returned. "It's nobody's business how many names I have."

"Especially mine." I couldn't keep the sarcasm from my voice.

"You said it, not me." Nancy put her jacket on. "I'm going home. The atmosphere isn't so friendly around here."

I didn't stop Nancy and apologize to her.

Nancy makes me so mad, acting so secretive about her pledge sheet. That, on top of Gram's news, is too much. Gram and Nancy seem to be on the same side. Gram even told Nancy about her plans before she told her own family.

And they both seem to be against me.

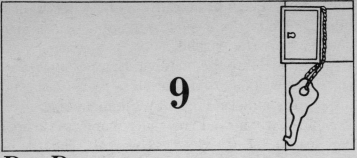

**9**

**D**ear **D**iary:

I didn't sleep at all last night, Diary. I felt terrible about the fight Nancy and I had.

This morning I overslept, which meant I didn't have time for breakfast. I ran out the door, hoping to catch Nancy before she left.

I was too late — Nancy had already left on her bike. I ended up half-running to school, but I made it before the first bell.

Nancy was locking her bike to the rack outside the front doors. She looked at me puffing toward her, then looked away again.

"I'm sorry," I said immediately. "I was in a bad mood last night because of Gram. But I shouldn't have taken it out on you."

Nancy gave her lock a final tug to make sure it was secure. "It's okay," she said. "I shouldn't have snapped at you."

"I guess we were both to blame," I said, relieved we were still friends. Nancy was so strange these days, I couldn't be sure. "I hate it when we fight."

"Me, too," she agreed.

We walked into the building. Ericka Powell and some other kids from our class were gathered around the bulletin board by the main office.

A big chart showed how much money the school had raised for Children's Hospital. The sixth-grade car wash and the fifth-grade bake sale had been held over the weekend. The fourth-grade lawn-raking project ended when we had our first snow. Our class had the only blank space on the chart. The Read-A-Thon was still two days away.

"We'll make more money than Mr. Devon's class did," Ericka remarked, slipping her knapsack off her shoulder. "They only made twenty-six dollars and fourteen cents. I have more than that in pledges."

"So do I," I said. "And Nancy does, too, don't you, Nancy?" Actually, I didn't know how many pledges Nancy had signed up — her pledge sheet could be in Kalamazoo, for all I knew.

Instead of answering, Nancy did the dumbest thing. She grabbed Ericka's knapsack and threw it to Tanya Malone. "Let's play Keep Away!" she yelled. Giggling, Tanya tossed the knapsack over Ericka's head back to Nancy.

"Give it here!" Ericka demanded, trying to reach her knapsack. Nancy was so tall, it was like jumping for the moon.

"Nancy!" I shouted. "Give it back to her. Stop acting like a little kid."

Just then the office door opened. Mr. Rice came out. He frowned when he realized his students were the cause of all the racket. Nancy gave Ericka her knapsack with a sheepish grin.

"I hope you people behave more seriously Wednesday," Mr. Rice said.

Ericka and Tanya drifted down the hall toward our classroom. The bell was about to ring so I started walking in that direction, too. Nancy hung back.

"Mr. Rice," I heard her say nervously. "About Wednesday — "

Whatever Nancy was going to ask him was drowned out by the arrival of Samantha Howard. Jessica and Candace were right behind her.

"Mr. Rice!" Samantha cried, ignoring Nancy. "Do you have any news yet?"

"About the dance?" Mr. Rice replied. "Mr. Devon and I brought it up at a meeting. The principal said he'd think it over."

Samantha could barely contain her excitement. "He'll say yes, won't he, Mr. Rice? He's just got to! Next time you see him, tell him I'll do all the work. Everything. You teachers won't have to lift a finger."

Mr. Rice smiled wryly. "That'll be a first, but I appreciate your offer. I'll be sure to tell the principal the students really want a dance."

"Everybody wants it," Samantha declared. "It'll be the greatest thing the sixth grade ever did."

"Well, we'll just have to wait and see what the principal says." Mr. Rice picked up his pace, our signal to hurry and get to class.

Nancy caught up with me. She must have been as surprised about the news of the dance as I was.

Samantha started to push past us. That made me angry. She had the whole hall. She didn't have to make us move.

"Who says everybody wants a dance?" I demanded. "Just because *you* want one, doesn't mean everybody else does."

Samantha gave me a long cool stare. "Everybody who *counts* wants a dance. The babies can go play with the kindergarteners."

"Are you calling us babies?" I said defensively.

"I really don't have time for this." Samantha sailed ahead of me and Nancy. Her friends followed her, giggling.

"That girl makes me so mad!" I said, gritting

my teeth. "She thinks she owns the world!"

In a way, Samantha *does* own the world. Nancy and I don't call her Queen of the Sixth Grade for nothing. That's what *really* makes me mad. I don't have one tenth of the control Samantha has in her little finger.

I knew, Diary, it was time to write the last note. I wanted my grand moment of triumph over the Queen.

After calling the roll, Mr. Rice put an assignment on the board and told us to work quietly on our own. We were supposed to answer questions at the end of the Stories from Far-Away Lands in our reading books.

Instead, I wrote the final love letter to Samantha from her secret admirer. I feel a little guilty when I do personal stuff in class. But I knew the questions wouldn't take too long to answer, and the letter was more important.

"I just wrote the last note to Samantha," I whispered to Nancy when I had finished. "Her secret admirer wants to reveal his identity, so he's arranged a meeting. Isn't that cool? All I have to do is deliver the note and get her to the right place at the right time."

"How are you going to deliver this one?" Nancy asked. "First-grade messenger? Or the mailbox trick?"

"Samantha can't suspect it's anybody from our school," I said. "I'm pretty sure she believes her secret admirer is Adam, especially after what happened the other day." I had told Nancy about Samantha trying to get Adam to pledge for the Read-A-Thon so she could have his signature. "So I guess I'll use the mailbox trick again. I'll have to be extra careful that she doesn't see me. I don't suppose you'd like to volunteer?" I added half-heartedly. Nancy lives closer to Samantha than I do.

"Sure. You have the note all written and everything, don't you?"

I nearly fell out of my chair. This was the first time since I came up with my plan that Nancy had agreed to help me. I passed her the envelope. "Don't let anybody see you. Come by my house when you're finished, okay?"

Nancy tucked the envelope in her pocket. At the front of the room, Samantha, the unsuspecting victim, whispered something to Candace. Nancy grinned at me. I grinned back. It was going to work!

"There is entirely too much noise in here," Mr. Rice said, getting up from his desk. He looked around the classroom, searching for the talkers. His gaze rested on Nancy. "Ms. Underpeace."

When he used our last names, he meant business. "I believe I heard your voice."

"It wasn't just me," Nancy said defensively. "Other people were talking just as much." She stared at Samantha and Candace, who both acted innocent.

It never did any good to point this out to Mr. Rice. "I gave you an assignment to work on *quietly*. Since you can't do that, we'll do the assignment in class." Everyone groaned. "Nancy," Mr. Rice said. "Read question number one and answer it."

Nancy jumped up. She always got really nervous when she had to read out loud. She picked up her textbook and held it in front of her as if she had suddenly gone blind. " 'What . . . is . . . the . . . p-p-p — ' "

" 'Purpose,' " I coached her.

Her book crashed to the floor. Samantha jumped as if she'd been shot. Jessica and Donald laughed.

"Sorry." Nancy stooped to pick it up.

Mr. Rice simply waited for her to find her place and go on, instead of letting someone else answer the way he sometimes did.

After several seconds of page flipping, Nancy said, "Well, everybody knows the question. I'll just answer it. Uh . . . the story was about this kid — "

"Boy or girl?" Mr. Rice interrupted.

My book was open to the story. Above the title was an illustration of a boy climbing a mountain. Nancy sneaked a quick glance.

"Boy," she said. "Anyway, this boy climbs this mountain and — and he gets stuck on the top without any food or water — "

I shook my head wildly. None of that was in the story! Nancy was making it up!

Mr. Rice figured it out, too. "Nancy, did you read the story or are you guessing?"

"I read it, " Nancy said quickly. "I just forgot. Didn't we read it a long time ago?"

"Last week. Surely your memory isn't that short."

"My mother says I'd forget my head if it wasn't tied on," she joked. Some of the kids laughed.

Mr. Rice told her to sit down, then called on Donald Harrington. Nancy pretended to wipe sweat off her forehead. I noticed she really was sweating — her upper lip was moist. I can't understand it. Nancy's grades aren't the greatest, but actually, she's very smart. She just never shows it in class.

At lunch I went over the final details of my plan. "Samantha's secret admirer wants to meet her tomorrow after school," I said. "He's supposed to meet her at four-thirty, outside Bentley's Ice-cream Parlor. We'll be hiding behind the trees across the street. It'll be a riot, Nance. I can't wait!"

Nancy paused, her sandwich halfway to her mouth. "Tomorrow afternoon? I thought it was this afternoon."

"That's when you deliver the note," I told her. "Samantha might not get it until late this evening. I had to make the meeting a day from the time she received the note."

"I can't be there."

"What do you mean, you can't be there?"

"I have an appointment."

"Can't you break it?" I asked, feeling annoyed. "This is really important."

"So is my appointment," she said. "I can't miss it. Especially this week."

Angrily I stabbed my straw into my juice carton. "How come *I* don't know anything about these mysterious appointments?"

She shrugged. "I guess you don't know everything about me, Lizzie Miletti."

"I guess you aren't interested in being my friend anymore, either! When we get back to class, give me the note," I demanded. "I'll deliver it to Samantha myself. I wouldn't want to bother you."

Then I grabbed my lunch and stamped over to the table where Ericka and Tanya were sitting. They yakked about the Read-A-Thon, but I just ate. My sandwich tasted like sawdust.

What worries me is if Nancy wants to keep secrets from me, maybe she doesn't need a best friend!

Anyway, Nancy wasn't in school today. If she is sick, it must have been a sudden illness because she seemed fine yesterday. Except when we had our fight. After the argument at lunch, Nancy wordlessly put the note to Samantha on my desk and didn't look at me the rest of the afternoon.

I told myself I didn't care whether Nancy was sitting in the seat next to me or not. But I missed her. A lot.

The only good thing about the day was Samantha. She was on Cloud Nine. The instant I saw her I knew she had big plans for the afternoon.

For one thing, she was dressed up. She had on a new pink sweater with a lace collar and pale blue jeans with a matching short jacket. The back of the jacket was covered with funky pins.

She looked fabulous.

I could barely keep from giggling as I passed her desk. She had no idea that I, Elizabeth Jane Miletti, was about to play the biggest joke on her in history. Too bad Nancy had to miss it. Then I remembered Nancy wouldn't have been able to go anyway. She had her secret appointment.

Mr. Rice collected our pledge sheets. The Read-A-Thon was tomorrow. Four people had pledged the full amount on my sheet, ten dollars for seventy-five pages, plus six smaller pledges. I wasn't sure how much money in pledges Nancy had signed up. She'd turn her sheet in late, if she could find it. At least a couple of her pledges were for ten dollars, too.

When the last bell rang I purposely took a long time to pack my knapsack. I wanted to give Samantha a head start. Samantha bolted for the girls' room, with Candace and Jessica right behind her.

Outside, Jessica and Candace waved good-bye. Samantha walked down the street alone, hurrying to meet her secret admirer. I followed at a safe distance behind so she wouldn't be suspicious.

Samantha got to Bentley's Ice-cream Parlor and looked up and down the street. When she didn't see anyone who could be her secret admirer, she pulled a mirror from her purse and began primping.

Using the trees for cover, I found a hiding place across the street. I could see Samantha but she couldn't see me.

I yanked my knit hat over my ears. It was cold today. Samantha wasn't even wearing a hat. No doubt she didn't want to mess up her gorgeous hair. In fact, she wasn't wearing anything but that skimpy jeans jacket with the pins on the back. She was probably freezing.

This was absolutely perfect, I thought happily. I couldn't have dreamed a better scene. Samantha was going to wait and wait and *wait* for Adam to show up and confess he was her secret admirer. She was going to freeze to death. I know it was mean, but what she did to me was mean, too. Asking me to have a slumber party and then ruining it on purpose. And she was going to feel like a first-class idiot when *I* emerged from my hiding place and announced the joke.

If only Nancy had been with me to witness my grand moment. But we weren't speaking to each other. I put Nancy out of my mind, the way I put Gram out of my mind.

Across the street Samantha paced impatiently. She kept checking her watch and flapping her arms to stay warm.

I wondered how long I should make her wait. I didn't want her to come down with pneumonia. Still it wouldn't hurt her to get the sniffles. I'd love to see beautiful Samantha Howard with a red nose. I know that sounds mean, Diary, but Samantha does that to me.

She tapped her foot. I could tell she was really antsy. Before I made my dramatic appearance, I had to practice what I would say. A grand moment required a little speech.

I could say, "April Fool!" but it was the wrong month.

Or I could say, "Waiting for somebody, Samantha?" And when she said yes, I'd quote from the first note in this high-pitched voice, "I have watched you from afar with a heavy heart — "

Then she'd know instantly I was the one who wrote the notes.

It was time.

I stepped from the bushes and waited until the traffic cleared.

Then I saw him.

Billy Watts, the cutest boy in the entire sixth-grade class. Billy is a million times cuter than Donald Harrington. Most of the girls are in love with Billy.

And here he was, stopping to talk to Samantha Howard!

I couldn't hear what they were saying, but he seemed glad to see her. She looked positively thrilled to see him! Who wouldn't be? They chatted a few minutes and then — would you believe this, Diary — they walked into Bentley's! Samantha hung onto Billy's arm as if he had just rescued her from a shipwreck.

I raced across the street and leaned against the cold plate glass. Inside, a waitress led the couple to an empty booth.

Samantha faced the window. She was grinning like somebody who'd won the lottery. In a way, she had.

I guess she believed everything had all fallen into place. Her secret admirer wasn't Adam after all, but Billy Watts. Billy could easily have gotten a first-grader to deliver his first note to Samantha. And since he lived fairly close, he could have put the other letters in her mailbox.

Then I realized that if Samantha talked about the letters, Billy wouldn't know what she was talking about. He'd think she was crazy. I thought, but maybe she won't say anything about the love letters. Samantha is pretty smart. She wouldn't ruin her chance with the cutest guy in the school.

And *I* had thrown them together. Brilliant move!

Just then Samantha glanced up and saw me peering in the window. Smiling, she waved.

I turned in disgust to walk home. I'll probably

never get even with Samantha now. Whoever said revenge was sweet told a big fat lie. Revenge tastes sour and bitter.

Diary, I wasted *weeks* on my plan to get back at Samantha. And for what? Samantha is now with the boy *I* like. My best friend will probably never speak to me again. And I still don't have any control over my own life.

In fact, I feel like I'm going backwards. I guess I'm doing something wrong.

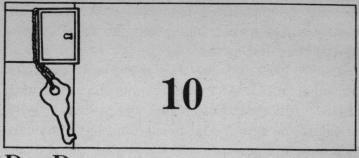

**10**

Dear Diary:

I hardly recognized Mr. Rice's classroom when I walked in. It had been transformed for Read-A-Thon day.

Instead of the usual neat rows, the desks were grouped around the room. Brightly colored pillows and cushions were on the seats of the desk and in between on the floor. A fat green beanbag chair sat under the window like a frog.

The blackboard had been completely erased except for the word "READ" in gigantic multi-colored letters. Two library carts jammed with books stood in front of Mr. Rice's desk.

Mr. Rice had filled little plastic bowls with pretzels, nuts, and M&M's. He had on a red jogging suit and tennis shoes. "Wear comfortable clothes," he'd advised us yesterday. "You'll be sitting and reading all day."

We wore the same clothes we wear every day, jeans and sweaters or sweatshirts. Mr. Rice was the only one who had to change from what he usually wore, which was a suit and tie. I had on my softest jeans and a big slouchy sweatshirt I borrowed from Josh. He said I stole it but I told him he could have it back any time he wanted. That doesn't make it stealing.

"Who gets the beanbag chair?" Donald Harrington wanted to know immediately. As if only the privileged should sit there — like him.

"We all do," Mr. Rice replied. "We'll take turns. Twenty minutes at a time."

Everyone was excited. It was like a party. Mr. Rice set the bowls of snacks around the room. He put a bowl of pretzels on my desk, and I felt very lucky. After a steady diet of Roth's frozen zucchini-and-pea sticks, pretzels were a real treat.

"These aren't all for you," Mr. Rice told me with a wink. To the class he said, "Feel free to sit anywhere you like. On the floor, in a chair. You don't have to sit in your assigned seats today."

"I can't even *find* mine," Donald said, but I could tell he wasn't complaining. This was going to be a fun day.

Mr. Rice went to the door to call the stragglers hanging around in the hall before first bell. "We need to take roll call and then get started."

Samantha Howard was one of the stragglers, and I saw why. Billy Watts walked her to the door. He said something that made her laugh. She looked like one of those pretty girls in a breath mint ad, radiant and happy. Every girl in the room gawked at them. And every girl in the room, including me, was envious. Seeing Samantha with the cutest boy in the school reminded me how totally my plan had failed. I felt terrible all over again.

Nancy was late. I hadn't called her because I was so depressed. But now I was anxious to make up with her and tell her what had happened.

"Isn't Billy sweet?" Samantha squealed when she found Jessica and Candace, who had staked out a group of desks near the windows.

"Adorable," Mr. Rice said wryly. "If you don't mind, Samantha, we have a Read-A-Thon to conduct today."

Samantha slid gracefully into her seat. "Of course," she said smoothly. She was so sure of herself, as always. And why shouldn't she be, with her looks and now the cutest boy in the entire school?

Mr. Rice quickly took attendance. When he got to the last name, Nancy's, he looked up. "Is Nancy out sick again, does anyone know? Lizzie?"

Before I could answer, Robert Wilkins spoke up. "I saw her bike in the rack," he said. "So she's here."

Mr. Rice frowned. "I wonder why she's not in her seat. Lizzie, would you go look for her? She might be in the girls' room." He gave me the big wooden key that we use as a hall pass. "Don't take too long. We must get started. Your goal is seventy-five pages, remember."

"I picked out some good books so it should be easy," I said. But I was really worried. Where was Nancy? If her bike was in the rack outside, why wasn't she in the classroom? Maybe she was sick or hurt someplace!

Guilt jabbed me like a needle as I ran down the hall. I knew I should have called her last night to see how she was. Who cared if my dumb old revenge plan failed? It wasn't important. My best friend was probably very sick, and I hadn't even bothered to call her. I guess I'm not a very nice person.

Just to make sure Robert wasn't mistaken, I ran to the front door and checked the bike rack. Sure enough, Nancy's bike was there.

Then I ran to the girls' room. No one was standing in front of the sinks. But the stall door on the one end was closed. I heard faint sobs. Someone was in there . . . crying.

"Nancy?" My voice bounced off the tiled walls. "Is that you?"

The sobs stopped abruptly, then the door unbolted. Nancy came out. Her eyes were swollen and red. She looked awful.

"Nancy!" I cried. "What's wrong? Are you sick? Do you want me to get the nurse?"

She shook her head. "Oh, Lizzie, I don't know what I'm going to do! I can't go to class. I tried to stay home again today but Mom made me come. She didn't really believe I had a sore throat yesterday."

I was confused. "You weren't sick yesterday?"

"No. Not *that* kind of sick. But I'm so scared, I feel sick." She clutched her stomach with both hands. "I don't know what I'm going to do."

"Nancy, what *is* it?" Something terrible was wrong with my friend.

She bit her bottom lip. "I'm not sure I want to tell you."

"Please tell me," I pleaded. "I can't help you if you won't tell me what's wrong."

"You can't help me," she said bleakly. "Nobody can." She started to cry again, huge gulping sobs.

I was afraid she'd *really* be sick, so I ran cold water over paper towels folded into a thick pad. "Here. Put this on your head. It'll make you feel better." Then I went into the stall and got a wad of toilet paper so she could blow her nose.

The cold towel seemed to help. After a few minutes, Nancy's sobs slowed.

"You're missing the Read-A-Thon," she snuffled.

"It's okay. I can read my pages in no time. I hope some pretzels are left," I added, trying to make her laugh. "Do you feel like going back to class now?"

Her mouth tightened. "I can't, Lizzie. It'll be too embarrassing."

"*What* will be embarrassing? Will you *tell* me?"

She shredded the paper towel into wet crumbs. "All right. I can't believe you haven't guessed anyway, after all these years."

"Guessed what?" I was frightened. Was Nancy seriously ill? I remembered a kid in fourth grade who had to go to the hospital a lot.

She looked at me unblinkingly. "I can't read," she stated.

"Can't read?" I repeated. "Of course you can read. You're in the sixth grade, Nancy. How could you get promoted if you can't read?"

She leaned against the sink, staring at the green-and-white tiled floor. "I have a, a — learning disability. I can't read, and I can't write very well, either. And other things are hard to do — like telling time."

"But I've *seen* you read!" I protested.

"No, I open books but I don't read them," she corrected miserably. "I don't see words when I look at a page. I see — jumbled-up letters. Like a secret code . . . or a foreign language. I can read a little, but it takes me forever. And even then I get the words wrong half the time. The same with writing. I'll do *anything* to keep from writing in class."

I remembered a half a dozen small scenes in the class. Nancy sharpening her pencil over and over. Fiddling with her hair, gazing out the window. Pretending she didn't hear the assignment. Whenever Mr. Rice asked her to read out loud, she *did* get the words wrong. Everybody would laugh and she'd act like she did it on purpose, made a joke. The incidents added up — Nancy was telling the truth.

"Oh, Nancy." I thought my friend had complete control over her life. Was I ever wrong!

"You don't know what it's been like," she went on. "Kids calling me dummy. Feeling stupid. And reading out loud is awful. The very worst."

"But Nancy, you pass tests," I said. "How could you do that if you can't read?"

"I can read, some. But I have to do it my way. I do okay on tests because I memorize things. I have a great memory. It's doing things like writing in class that's so hard."

No wonder she didn't want anything to do with my love-letter scheme. Writing her own papers was tough enough. And I had asked her to copy over a bunch of letters! Some friend I was.

"If we're allowed to take work home, Mom helps me," Nancy said. "That's why I always turn my papers in late. So she can help me."

"Then your mom knows you have this — learning thing?"

"It's called dyslexia. Yeah, she knows. She was the one who got me the special teacher I go to twice a week. I've been going since school started."

That explained Nancy's mysterious appointments. "Why didn't you *tell* me?" I asked.

Her eyes were suddenly dark. "Would you have listened?"

Her statement hit home. I *had* been too busy with my own problems, worrying about Gram and trying to get even with Samantha.

"I'm sorry," I told her. "I wish — well, I'm just sorry."

"It's okay."

But it really wasn't okay and we both knew it. A person did not let her best friend walk around miserable for weeks — years, even — and not notice.

"What about Mr. Rice?" I asked. "Does he know about your — problem?"

She shook her head. "I started to tell him the other day. But I don't want *any*body to know. Except you. Promise you won't tell anybody."

"Maybe if Mr. Rice knew you had dyslexia, he'd be easier on you in class."

"I want to be treated like everybody else," Nancy insisted stubbornly. "I don't want to go to the dummy reading class again." Nancy was always in the lowest reading group. And last year she had gone to Ms. Carroll, the reading specialist.

I touched her arm. "Nancy, we'd better get back. Mr. Rice sent me to find you."

"I can't go!" she wailed. "I can't read that big thick book I checked out of the library! I can't read anything under pressure! All those people who signed my pledge sheet — "

The Read-A-Thon. It must seem like a nightmare to Nancy. Now I understood why Nancy kept "losing" her pledge sheet. The last thing she needed was to have people pay her to read, even for a good cause. I could have kicked myself for all the times I said that reading was easy as pie.

"My teacher is helping me, but I'm still a dummy," she whispered.

I hugged her fiercely. "You are not a dummy, Nancy Underpeace. You're so smart it scares me sometimes. You knew all along my plan to get even with Samantha would flop."

"The meeting didn't work out?" she asked through her tears.

"You wouldn't believe how it backfired!" But we had a more important problem to solve.

"Listen," I said, "if you don't make your goal, it won't hurt anything."

"Everybody will meet their goal," Nancy said acidly. "Reading is easy for you guys. I'll be the only one to ruin the Read-A-Thon."

"We can't stay in here all day. Come on." I took Nancy's arm and led the way out into the hall. Mr. Rice was heading in our direction. Nancy looked like a frightened rabbit.

"I was about to send the secretary in there after you two," he said. "What's going on? Nancy, are you all right?"

She wasn't, but I knew Nancy would rather die than tell him. Still, Nancy couldn't go on pretending she could read when she couldn't. It wasn't fair to her, or to the teacher. Mr. Rice was cool. I was sure he'd be on her side.

"Nancy has dyslexia," I blurted suddenly. Nancy shot me a look that would definitely kill. "She has trouble reading," I went on before I lost my nerve. "She's scared to go to class."

Mr. Rice's features softened. "Ah," he said. "This explains your behavior in class. I suspected you might have a learning disability. You've been very good at hiding it."

"I'm going to a special teacher," Nancy said. "She's helping me, but — "

Mr. Rice put his arm around her shoulder. "But you still have to read today. I understand. How about if I — "

"I don't want to be excused. I want to be like everybody else . . . only I'm not," she added in a small voice.

I couldn't stand to see my best friend so miserable. She'd been through so much, trying to disguise the fact she couldn't read.

"I'll read Nancy's quota," I said without thinking. "I'll read hers and mine both. That way she'll be able to collect her pledges. And we won't tell anybody."

Mr. Rice stared at me. "Nancy is supposed to read seventy-five pages, Lizzie. And so are you. That's a hundred and fifty pages in one day. Can you do it?"

I wasn't at all sure I could. I am a good reader but not *that* good.

"You'd do that for me?" Nancy exclaimed in wonder. "You're going to read a hundred and fifty pages for me?"

My friendship with Nancy was at stake. If I failed, then I had blabbed Nancy's secret for nothing. She had every right to be mad at me for the rest of my life.

I smiled weakly. "What are friends for?"

Mr. Rice herded us back to the classroom. "I'll keep distractions away from you," he promised me. "And I won't tell anyone else what you're doing. It'll be our secret."

Everyone was busy reading when we entered the room. Some at their desks, some sprawled on the floor. Samantha Howard had claimed the green beanbag chair, naturally.

I didn't have time to think about Samantha. I went straight to the library cart and retrieved my three books. Nancy pulled out the big thick science book she had chosen. She stuck the little Beatrix Potter book in her pocket so no one would see it.

We took seats near the back corner. I opened *Little Women* and began reading as if my life depended on it. In a way, it did. Not my life, exactly, but my friendship with Nancy. I had let her down all these weeks, nagging her about her mysterious appointments and getting angry when she wouldn't copy my "secret admirer" letters. I felt ashamed.

The morning sped by. Howie Strauch's mother came in to take photographs for the *Hampton Point Marketplace*. Every half hour, Mr. Rice let us walk around the room for five minutes to talk and eat munchies. I stayed in my seat, reading. By lunchtime I had read four chapters of *Little Women*, a total of fifty pages. It was tough going — the print was small and, even though the story was interesting, it was taking me forever to finish a page. Now I knew how Nancy felt.

She propped up the big thick science book and put the little Beatrix Potter book inside it. She read very slowly, moving her lips to sound out each syllable.

We ate lunch we'd brought from home in our room. Mr. Rice supplied bottles of soda and fruit juice and a big platter of brownies.

"How are you doing?" Nancy asked me. "Are you going to make it?"

I had serious doubts. In another hour or so, I would meet my own goal, but I didn't think I could meet Nancy's, too. I decided to tell Mr. Rice to mark Nancy's full quota and however many pages

I managed to read for myself. I was disappointed that I wouldn't be able to collect all those ten-dollar pledges for Children's Hospital, but even more worried about my friendship with Nancy.

Putting *Little Women* down, I switched to the Nancy Drew. It was easier to read and went much faster. By the one-thirty break, my eyes were bothering me. And I had a headache. I nibbled a pretzel and sipped some fruit juice. I had read a total of seventy-three pages.

A lot of kids were finished. At every break, Mr. Rice gave out more of the mimeographed "certificates" that proved we had reached our goal. We would need those certificates when we went around to collect the money from the people who pledged. Mr. Rice signed each certificate and pasted a big gold star on the top, to make it official.

Samantha got her certificate and pranced around the class, waving it like a flag. Those makeup books she checked out were the simplest things in the world to read.

By two-thirty nearly everyone was finished. The class was pretty noisy, waiting for the three o'clock bell. Mr. Rice told some kids, including Samantha and her friends, to start cleaning up. He came back to our corner.

"It's almost time for the bell," he told us. "How many pages have you read, Lizzie?"

Avoiding Nancy's eyes, I mumbled, "Only a hundred and four. I didn't make it, Mr. Rice. I'm really sorry."

"This is between us," Mr. Rice said confidentially, "but I took the liberty of reading some pages for you. After all, it's for a good cause. Add thirty pages, which brings the total to — a hundred and thirty-four."

"It's still not enough," I said glumly.

"Wait!" Nancy cried. "Look, I read to here." She showed Mr. Rice her place in the book.

"Page forty-three," he observed. "Well — "

"But half the pages are pictures," Nancy pointed out honestly.

Mr. Rice smiled. "Even taking that into account, you reached your goals, with five pages to spare! Congratulations!" With a flourish, he signed our certificates.

Nancy threw her arms around me in a bear hug. "We did it! We did it!"

"You mean, you're not mad at me because I didn't read all those pages for both of us, like I promised?" I said.

"We worked as a team," Nancy replied jubilantly. "And that's how it should be. It's going to be that way from now on. No more secrets."

"No more secrets," I agreed emphatically.

My eyes were hurting me but I felt terrific.

Nancy and I were friends again. Real, true, do-anything-for-each-other best friends.

At the front of the room, Mr. Rice flicked the lights on and off to get the class's attention.

"The Read-A-Thon is officially over," he announced. "Every single one of you met your reading goals! Give yourselves a great big cheer."

Everybody yelled. Samantha clasped her hands over her head in a winner's gesture, as if she accomplished the whole thing herself. Suddenly I didn't care if I ever got even with the Queen of the Sixth Grade. Other things were more important.

"You know," I said to Nancy. "Revenge isn't sweet at all. It's dumb. Don't you think so?"

Nancy didn't answer. She was looking at her certificate with the big gold star at the top, and beaming.

You know, Diary, I felt the way I did when I helped Darcy make Christmas presents. I forgot all about my problems that night, probably because I was concentrating on making somebody else happy.

I feel that way now. Only better.

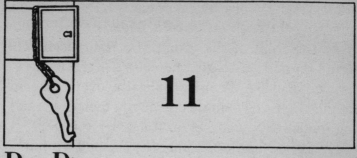

**11**

**D**ear **D**iary:

After school Nancy and I went around the neighborhood to collect our pledge money. Nancy was so proud of her certificate. I bet she showed it to my mother fifty times. My mom just smiled, but Gram declared a celebration was in order and went out to buy a cake from the bakery. I think Gram knew about Nancy's problem. I *should* have known but I didn't because I've been too wrapped up in my own problems. I plan to be a better friend from now on, Diary.

Nancy stayed for supper. Gram's cake reminded us that our class raised more money for Children's Hospital than any other class in the entire school.

Josh toasted us with his milk glass. "To the fastest readers in Claremont!"

Nancy and I just looked at each other. Well, maybe we weren't the fastest readers, but together we made a pretty good team.

Mrs. Underpeace, who had worked late, came

over to pick Nancy up. "How was your big day?" she asked Nancy. "I wanted to call this afternoon, but I knew you and Lizzie would be out collecting money!"

"You'll never guess!" Nancy danced around her mother with her certificate. "If you read all your pages, you got one of these. Lizzie helped me reach my goal and Mr. Rice gave me a certificate, too."

"She earned it," I said truthfully. "We both read today until our eyes practically dropped on the floor."

Mrs. Underpeace gave Nancy a squeeze. "Oh, honey, I'm so proud of you."

"Mr. Rice knows about my dyslexia," Nancy confessed. "I couldn't keep it from him any longer. I had to tell him."

"I think it's best," her mother said. To me she said, "Nancy's dyslexia was diagnosed late this summer, and that's when we found Nancy the special tutor. I wanted to tell Nancy's teachers, but Nancy didn't want anyone to know. Now she can get help from both her tutor and your teacher."

"And catch up twice as fast," I put in.

Nancy grinned. "Who knows? Maybe I'll be able to read that big, thick science book soon. I can't wait to read it out loud in class. I'll bet old Donald

Harrington won't make fun of me then!"

They left, Nancy talking happily about the number of pages she had read to help raise money for Children's Hospital. I watched them walk down the street arm in arm, their breath making frosty puffs in the night air. They seemed to have so much to say to each other. I envy Nancy. Her parents really love her. My family loves me, too, but things haven't been the same in our house since Gram began dating Mr. Bagnold.

Friday was our last day of school before the holidays.

"I have an announcement," Mr. Rice said. "The principal has given permission for a sixth-grade dance in the spring — "

Cheers interrupted the rest of his announcement, but there were some boos. Nancy was one of the booers.

"Don't you want a dance?" I asked her.

"Are you kidding? Dancing is so dumb." She wrinkled her nose. "I'd rather have a party at the arcade. Something fun. Wouldn't you?"

I felt both scared and excited. Mostly scared, I think. I can dance a little, but I don't know if I could remember how if a boy actually asked me to dance. Even worse, suppose *nobody* asks me to dance!

At least the dance is a long way off, in the spring. I won't have to worry about it for months.

Samantha looked extra smug. She'd won again, but then she always does.

Mr. Rice collected our pledge money, and then we had a pizza party. Candace's mother brought in cupcakes decorated with crushed candy canes. "Candy canes for Candy," Donald chortled, as if he'd thought of something original. There were enough cupcakes to go around, so I wasn't asked if I minded not having one. Maybe my life is starting to improve, finally. Oh, Diary, how I hope that's true!

The last few days before Christmas have been pretty crazy in the Miletti house.

We all had a million jobs to do. Our kitchen was like an all-night diner — it never closed. When Mom wasn't cooking our regular meals, she was making Jello-O salads and casseroles. Both Mom and Gram were beginning to look frazzled. And they didn't say much to each other, either.

Early Christmas Eve morning, Nancy called me. "Your grandmother said Oscar is old enough for me to take home. Mom said I could get him tonight, if that's okay. Can we come over around eight-thirty?"

"Sure." I'd probably be thrilled to have some

company by then. Without Gram, it was going to be a very gloomy evening.

Before lunch, Gram came downstairs with her overnight case and a big shopping bag. She was wearing a new beige suit that made her look very pretty. But the corners of her mouth kept twitching, as if she were trying not to cry.

"Well, everybody," she said with false brightness. "I'll see you the day after tomorrow. Have a — wonderful Christmas."

"I hope you like what I got you, Gram," Darcy said shrilly. "I made it all by myself."

That wasn't exactly true. I had helped Darcy. But I'd never give away her secret. Maybe one day I won't have any secrets to guard or find out.

"I'm sure I'll love it, honey," Gram stooped to kiss Darcy and Rose again.

"Will you call us?" Darcy asked.

Gram straightened, her eyes shiny. "Of course I'll phone."

"Lizzie," Mom said meaningfully. "Gram is waiting to leave."

I stumbled across the rug and kissed Gram's cheek. She smelled of lilies of the valley, her favorite perfume. Her cheek was soft as velvet. I loved my grandmother so much, I knew I was going to cry.

"Merry Christmas, dear," she whispered.

I was too choked up to say anything. Instead I backed away like a wooden soldier. I wouldn't let Gram see me cry. She was doing this to us, we weren't doing anything to her.

Mr. Bagnold pulled up in his big blue car. I recognized the noisy engine. Gram looked at us one more time, then hurried outside before That Man could come to the door.

Christmas Eve supper wasn't nearly as dismal as Thanksgiving dinner had been. For one thing, it's not such a big deal. Mom fixed a ham and salads and rolls and put everything on the dining room table. We ate sitting around the tree in the living room.

We were almost finished eating when we heard noises outside — car doors slamming and people laughing. I thought it might be Nancy and her mother, but they would have walked. Plus it was too early.

Our front door burst open with a blast of cold air. Gram and Ralph Bagnold tumbled inside, laughing and dropping suitcases.

Mom stood riveted in shock. "Mother! What're you doing here?"

"Oh, Lynn, we've had such a time!" Gram replied. "The car broke down — "

"Right outside Detroit," Mr. Bagnold interrupted. "We've spent the whole evening getting it towed. The first tow truck they sent got lost or something — "

"It never came," Gram said, taking up the story. "So Ralph called again. The second one must have taken the Alaskan route."

"How did you get here?" Dad wanted to know.

"The gas station rented us a loaner," Mr. Bagnold answered. "Not very pretty but at least it runs!" He helped Gram with her coat, then handed Dad his hat. It looked as though they were going to stay. "I had the engine worked on not two weeks ago," he said to Dad, shaking his head.

"I don't understand," Mom said. "Why did you come back here? You had plans — "

"Oh, Lynn." Gram held my mother's hands in both of hers. "I want to be with my family. It occurred to me in that gas station. I thought to myself, 'Betty, why aren't you at home?' So Ralph brought me back."

Mom hugged her. "Mother, I'm so glad."

"Well, now that you're here, let's get this evening rolling," Dad said. "I was just about to whip up my famous eggnog. You're welcome to join us, Ralph."

"Don't mind if I do," Mr. Bagnold said, settling in the recliner with a relieved sigh.

Dad went into the kitchen to make his eggnog,

a drink nobody except grown-ups liked. Mom and I followed him, carrying plates and casserole dishes.

As I set a dish on the counter, I asked Mom, "Well, he's in our house. What are you going to do about it?"

Mom sliced a fruitcake. "Why, nothing, Lizzie. Why should I do anything about it?"

"I thought you didn't like him dating your mother." That was the impression she had given me for the past several weeks.

Mom paused, cake knife in midair. "I know. I've been acting very foolish. My mother is happy, and I'm glad for her." She handed me the platter of fruitcake to take into the living room.

I set the platter on the coffee table. Gram came over to me.

"Lizzie, how are you doing?"

"Okay," I fibbed. I'd been miserable all day, and it was her fault. Maybe my mother was happy for Gram, but I was still upset that Gram had almost ruined the holiday. "Are you going to be here tomorrow?" I asked pointedly.

"In the morning," she replied. "Ralph and I will go to his daughter's in the afternoon."

"What about your trip?"

"We canceled it. The people we were going to visit were very understanding, especially when

141

they found out we had car trouble. We'll go another time."

Dad and Mom came in with trays of punch cups brimming with the awful milky liquid. I took a cup, swapping a fake gag with Adam. He hated eggnog as much as I did.

Dad made a simple toast. "To families."

"To families," Gram echoed. "It means so much for me to be here, with the people I love."

Soon everybody was laughing and talking. They didn't need me. As soon as I could slip out unnoticed, I went to my room.

I was staring morosely out the window when someone tapped at my door.

"Come in," I said listlessly.

It was Gram. She had a present in her hand.

"It's not Christmas yet," I said, glancing at the gift.

"I won't tell if you won't," she said, smiling. "It'll be our secret."

I've had enough secrets lately. Nancy's secret, Gram's secret.

"Go on," Gram coaxed. "Open it, please. Make me happy."

I laughed, slipping the ribbon off. Then I gasped as I pulled the wrapping away.

It was a diary. The red leather cover had my name and the coming year stamped on it in gold letters. A tiny gold lock fastened the book shut, and a miniature key dangled from a red string. Unlocking the diary, I saw that the pages were undated, so I could write as much or as little as I wanted.

It was the perfect present. You, Diary, will run out in a few days, when this year ends. And now I have a new one. I'll always keep you, though.

"Oh, Gram," I whispered. "How did you know — ?"

"I think you're old enough to write down your thoughts," she said. "When I saw this, I knew it was for you."

She didn't know, then, that I was keeping a diary. But she sensed I *needed* a diary and she bought me one.

I hugged her. "I love it, Gram. I just — " I stopped, on the brink of tears.

Gram moved closer to me. "What is it, Lizzie?"

"You don't love us anymore," I said in a small voice, nervously pleating my bedspread. "You like Mr. Bagnold better than us."

She forced me to look at her. "Where on earth did you get such a notion?"

"You're always with him. You'd rather be with him than us."

"Oh, Lizzie," Gram sighed. "I like Ralph very much. And I do enjoy his company. But he and I learned something tonight. We both value our families and we have to be with them as well as with each other."

"You still love him more than us."

She pushed my bangs back. "You mean, more than you, don't you? I'll never love anybody the way I love my Elizabeth Jane. Can't you see that? That will never change."

"But things are different," I said.

"Yes," Gram agreed. "Things do change. That's what life is all about. Look at how your life changed this year."

"How?" My life was a complete drag. It wouldn't ever change for the better — I had no control over it.

Gram ticked the items off on her fingers. "You helped Nancy with her problems . . . you get along much better with your little sisters now, especially Darcy . . . you had a slumber party — "

"That disaster!"

"Maybe, but you learned how to handle a difficult situation," Gram pointed out. "You're learning about people, too. Yes, our lives are changing. We both have so much to look forward to," she concluded.

Maybe she did, but I didn't. I thanked her again for the diary. But I wonder if I'll have anything to write in it in the coming year.

*   *   *

The last day of the year.

It snowed again last night, but this morning the sun shone brightly through my bedroom curtains. The sky was blue, and the snow glittered like heaps of diamonds. It was going to be one of those sparkly winter days.

Nancy called right after breakfast. "Want to take a walk?" she asked.

"Okay," I agreed. "I'll meet you out front in half an hour." It would take that long to get bundled into my down jacket, mittens, scarf, hat, and snow boots. I hoped nobody yelled "Fire!" because I wouldn't be able to move too fast.

Nancy met me on my front steps. We began walking down the street. It was unbelievably quiet, except for some little kids building a snowman.

"How's Oscar?" I asked her. The other kittens were gone, too, given away to good homes. I actually missed the little puffs of fur running around.

"He slept curled up on my pillow last night," Nancy said. "He's so cute. Mom and I took pictures of him. A whole roll of film. I'm reading that book you loaned me. The one about cats? I'm only on page twelve, but so far it's pretty good."

I was glad that Nancy had found a book she liked to read. But I was even more glad that we

145

were friends again and that there were no secrets between us.

"You know, when you kept having those mysterious appointments, I was worried," I admitted. "I thought you might be sick. Or that you were tired of being friends with me."

"I'll never be tired of being friends with you," Nancy reassured me firmly. "We're best friends forever. And I didn't really like keeping a secret from you."

I dug my boot into a bank, dislodging a clump of snow. "It seemed like everybody had a secret from me. You, Gram, even my mother for a while. I hate secrets."

Nancy stopped to readjust her scarf. "You were keeping a secret, too, you know."

"I was?" How could I possibly have had a secret when I was so busy trying to find out everybody else's secrets?

"You had a secret from Samantha. You were really writing those letters, but the only person who knew it was me," she said.

As usual, Nancy was right. I was just as guilty as the others.

"No more secrets," I promised. And I meant it.

We reached the vacant lot. Supposedly a rich man owns the lot. He was going to build a fabulous house on it, but he never has. Everybody uses the lot as a sort of private park. Nancy often comes here to birdwatch — it's closer than the wildlife preserve.

In a clearing was a three-foot high circular wall of snow. Five boys were busily making snowballs, which they stockpiled in the center of the fort.

"Is that Donald Harrington?" Nancy asked, shielding her eyes from the glare. "It is. And Howie Strauch."

"I think that's Robert, too," I said. It was hard to tell — they all wore their hats pulled low. "And a couple of guys from Mr. Devon's class. We probably shouldn't hang around." The sight of that growing stack of snowballs was making me uneasy.

"One of those guys is Billy Watts," Nancy said.

My heart gave a little flip.

The boys noticed us then, and tossed a couple of snowballs.

"Hey!" Nancy cried. "Here come the real targets."

Samantha and her friends scuffed up the street, heading our way. Jessica and Candace were muffled to the eyes in hats and wool scarves. Samantha had on a blazing white ski parka. Her blonde hair streamed over the thrown-back fur-trimmed hood. She looked stunning.

"They must have heard the guys were here,"

Nancy observed. "Samantha can't miss a chance to flirt."

"Or show off a new outfit," I sighed. Now the guys wouldn't pay any attention to us, with Samantha on the scene.

Sure enough, snowballs began to fly through the air. Samantha and Jessica and Candace squealed and shrieked, but they didn't run. They *wanted* those guys to throw snowballs at them. Nancy tossed a couple and hit Donald in the ear, knocking his hat off. I didn't even try to throw a snowball. I have a terrible aim.

A snowball hit me square on the leg. I figured it was a stray.

"Billy threw that one at you," Nancy said. "He's getting ready to aim another one."

Whomp! The snowball hit my shin. "How come he has it in for me?" I wailed.

"He probably likes you," Nancy said out of the side of her mouth, winding up to pitch. "Don't boys do stupid things when they like a girl?"

I'd heard that, too, but I was surprised Nancy believed it. She didn't even like boys. Yet Billy Watts was definitely aiming all his snowballs at me. And not at Samantha.

"Hey, Billy!" Samantha called. I knew she was jealous! Of me! The boy she liked wasn't paying any attention to her!

I was so happy, I scooped up a big wet handful of snow and formed it into a ball. And then, with perfect control, I threw it at Nancy. It hit her on the arm. She laughed and threw one at me. And then we both laughed. Perfect friends. Then Billy threw another one at me!

Maybe, just maybe, I *am* going to have a lot to write about in my diary! My life *is* changing, as Gram said.

Good-bye, old Diary. And hello, new Diary, I can't wait to write in you.

Lizzie is excited about going to a *real* dance, but Nancy says *she* won't go! And that's not the only problem the two best friends are having! Read Dear Diary #3: *The Dance*.